"If you're fed up with unhinged bad guys, Lilith Saintcrow delivers kickass unhinged *good* guys—shapeshifting sci-fi berserkers who love nothing better than feeding steel-toed boots to fascists."
—**Cherie Priest, author of *Boneshaker***

"No punches pulled here: every gonzo scene is an amped-up, rocket-powered piledriver smashing straight into the slack-jawed face of fascism. They can run, but the little bitches can't hide."
—**Curtis C. Chen, award-winning author of the Kangaroo series**

"Lilith Saintcrow's *Coyote Run* does what it says on the tin: A near-future quasi-urban fantasy where the titular Coyote takes on fascists in a nearby state. The result is a balls-to-the-wall, pedal-beyond-the-metal-and-into-the-next-level novella that grabs the reader from the word go and does not let up to the finale. *Coyote Run* starts off with a crowd-pleasing bang and never relents. Come for the punching of fascists, stay for the strong characterization, rich worldbuilding, and intense action beats."
—**Paul "Princejvstin" Weimer, Hugo Award-Winning Fan Writer and Consumer of Words, Scion of St. Paul, Minnesota**

"Sometimes you just need to follow a bugfuck runner on a rescue op into fascist territory and watch her crack a few skulls. Actually, who am I kidding? We need stories like Saintcrow's all the time."
—**Brandon Crilly, award-winning author of the Aspects of Aelda**

COYOTE RUN

OTHER WORKS BY LILITH SAINTCROW

COYOTE RUN

AMAZING TALES **OF** ANTIFASCIST ACTION!

VOL. 1

LILITH SAINTCROW

Horned Lark Press

This is a work of fiction. All of the characters, organizations, and events portrayed in these stories are either products of the author's imagination or are used fictitiously.

Tacos are the best idea ever, though. That's nonfiction.

COYOTE RUN: AMAZING TALES OF ANTIFASCIST ACTION! VOL. 1

Coyote Run Copyright © 2025 by Lilith Saintcrow

Cover Art Copyright © 2025 by Phineas X. Jones

A Horned Lark Press Book

Published by Horned Lark Press
1087-2482 Yonge Street
Toronto, ON M4P 2H5

www.hornedlarkpress.com

2 4 6 8 9 7 5 3 1

First Edition

Print ISBN: 978-1-998390-12-0
Ebook ISBN: 978-1-998390-13-7

Printed in a Secret Volcano Lair by Antifascist Capybaras

For my grandfather, who went to war

PART ONE
THE PLAN

THE MUDHOLE

Most runners went to the Mudhole for a fight or a fuck, and the jobs offered there seemed largely incidental. Coyote, however, liked the drinks—strong enough to either kill a few neurons or disinfect engine parts.

Besides, when dumb assholes are fighting, a smart bitch can always pick up a few dropped trinkets.

A garish red neon Schlipperbier sign hung above the bar, a real vintage piece, pride and joy of the establishment. The weekday crowd was either lipwalking or busy striking deals, and it was relatively light—only two deep at the rail, skinny redheaded Pampier the head 'tender occasionally bawling explanatory or demanding obscenities over the noise, his two understudies moving so fast they nearly blurred.

From the small round table jammed under another glowing sign—blue LEDs cycling restlessly to spell out the name of a pisswater purveyor gone out of business long before the war's first shots were fired—Coyote had a good view of the entire bar. It wasn't prime real estate since the stench from the toilets down a short hall to her right was enough to give even a frontliner explosive nausea.

She could put her back to the wall and watch the action

anyway, while dialing down her nasal receptors. She'd smelled worse, and besides, the perch had an added benefit in cutting a lot of chitchat.

Right to business was the way Coyote liked it.

There were a few other shifters on deck tonight. Marbury the porcine slumped over a collection of shot glasses at the nearer end of the bar, his close-cropped, sweating head and prominent ivory teeth gleaming; the trio of large canids who ran military cargo were putting a dent in their most recent disbursement all the way across the Hole, not deigning to notice any smaller operators. There were even a couple soldiers with them, real jarhead types with combat implants probably thinking R&R spent with such riffraff would give them bragging rights when they went back to the front lines.

Coyote's lip lifted slightly.

The last shifter was the most interesting. She looked youngish, but that was no indication when you had a second skin. A mop of black hair only partially dyed with something strong enough to take root in robust shifter fur, nice wide hips just perfect for getting a grip on and a bust to match. Her overalls bore oil stains at the midriff where she'd lean against a transport, both knees, and the right thigh where she'd rub a paw after rummaging in an engine or other machinery. Well-worn plaid modcotton shirt underneath, and a pair of quality army-issues for hooves–if it was a disguise, it was a good one.

If it wasn't, she was a civilian wandering around the Mudhole, and that would only lead to trouble. Still, the civvie canvassed the entire bar twice, her long nose twitching a little, and her dark eyes were bright with intelligence.

Finally, she made up her mind and started her run. Beelined across the sticky floor in obvious fashion, in fact, walking straight for Coyote's table.

Great.

A rather large swallow of something impersonating bourbon went down easy, burning all the way. Coyote watched the civvie settle on the table's other stool, the rickety one that wasn't stolen by any regular in the crowd because of its visibly imperfect leg. The visitor frowned a little, that long nose wrinkling, and peered through the blue light.

"Fassby said you'd be here." At least she had enough sense not to yell, knowing Coyote's hearing was acute enough to catch a whisper even under the shouts, drunken laughter, and the sound system throbbing with Jute I's remix of Dillon's *Runner Blues*. "I'm Marge."

I do not fucking care. Coyote set her glass down, running a fingertip over the rim. Slightly damp, the bumps and divots of a mass-produced article undergoing hard use—a single-skin would only feel smooth glass. The poor ungifted fucks wandered around quarter-awake all the time, without even the sense God gave a sick armadillo.

Pointed chin jutting, Coyote scowled. Sand still lingered in her every crease—jeans, Federal Army surplus coat, boots, not to mention elbows, knees, and even behind her ears—from her last run, and her eyes bulged like boiled eggs. Her mouth was too wide and her hair a shaggy particolored mess, her ears impersonated jug handles and her front teeth crossed.

Nobody had made more successful crossings than her scrawny ass. It was even whispered she'd escaped a Lindyland chain gang or two, which was held to account for her usual sour temper.

Marge didn't fidget much, probably because the seat might collapse under her if she breathed wrong. "They say you take jobs nobody else will." Her hands lay flat on the table, and she'd have to wash them if she wanted to eat anything after this.

Who says? Coyote let her eyebrows rise a little. The other woman's nails were bitten down to the quick, but that was no indication. A shift's claws didn't depend on their weaker, blunted human form; control over shape and autonomics was the least of the gift.

"It's my sister." Marge's big brown eyes glistened; maybe the emotion was even real. A rough rasp of grief boiled under shitstink, carried from shifter-strong glands. "She's in a camp. Distarritz."

Oh, fuck. Coyote turned the glass a quarter of the way, the greasy ring underneath deforming like heat stress on an afterburner. Tapped her index finger twice, tiny unheard noises.

She could hop down from her own seat, Coyote supposed. Drain the liquor from her glass on the way to the bar, smack it down almost hard enough to break, and elbow her way to the door, maybe halting for two seconds to egg on a pair of highly sloshed bullet-eaters already yelling enthusiastically at each other in an ecstasy of incipient violence. Later she could tell Fassby to stop sending sob stories, too.

"I'm supposed to bring a shifter to trade for her." Marge blinked a couple times, and the swelling saltwater in her eyes could've been from the miasma drifting right into her face.

That was another reason Coyote chose this table. Lots of assholes lost interest when physical discomfort reached a certain pitch; it sifted out the committed from the day traders.

Finally, Coyote stirred again. "And you're tellin me this because..." Eyebrows hiked even more, one corner of her mouth twisting upward, her own fingernails thickening slightly. The points were sharp, triangular, and if she wanted to, she could peel a slice off the glass.

"Because I'm fuckin desperate." At least Marge was admitting it. "I want my sister back, someone's gotta know a way. Nobody will take this job unless I lie."

Now *there* was an interesting statement. If it was a con, it was a stupid one–or maybe that stupidity was just a veneer to make the mark feel smart.

Fuck it. Let's see what the fuck. "You got money?"

"I'm a mechanic, a good one. I'll work on any shit you bring me, priority, forever."

Not what I fuckin asked. "You got *money*?"

"Two hundred." And the civvie dug in an overalls pocket, the tip of that long nose wiggling. She blinked again, too, and Coyote realized she was probably myopic instead of dewy-eyed.

The dumbass was about to flash whatever pathetic wad she had in the middle of the Mudhole, not enough in cash or Federal chit to pay for even a short jaunt over the border but plenty to get shanked for in a barroom brawl. Coyote could already sense a few glances in their direction, and that was a bad sign.

Fucksake. "Hands on the desk, bitch," she snapped, and Marge's shoulders hunched. But she complied with reflexive speed, slapping her paws flat, and a few moments later she flinched when someone threw a bottle. The tinkling smash brought a torrent of blue language from Pampier, piercing the throbbing beat of Castillo's *Corrida Natural*.

There was going to be a melee in about fifteen standard seconds, Coyote could *smell* it. She tossed the rest of her drink down the hatch, tilted her head, and slid off her stool.

"Come on," she said, and headed down the hall for the back door next to the shitter.

FIXING CHICKEN

A convoy was thundering along Bascoe Road, troop carriers jammed with draftees about to do hard time on the front line, plus a long queue of supply haulers, their undersides glowing with antifrik cells. Coyote peered after them from the alley's dark toothless mouth, but most of her attention was on the shifter behind her.

Being able to look two ways at once was a prerequisite for runners, *if* they wanted to stay alive. A lot of shifters thought enhanced senses meant invulnerability, but it was easy to get sloppy from overload or sheer arrogance. There were a thousand ways to get fucked, even if the sainted Government Federal said shifters had the same rights as anyone else— including the right to be drafted and sent to hold the line against Lindbergh's bucket-helmeted jackholes.

Purebloods, Lindy's big blond clone-dicks called themselves, as if it meant anything other than a genetic dead end. Propaganda said the fash were finally on the run, but from what Coyote could tell the battle lines hadn't shifted in three long years and the current state of affairs was just to keep the masses clawing each other's eyes out instead of going after the profiteers keeping the whole damn dumbshow lurching along. Same type of fucks who paid for Lindbergh's rise to power thinking they could control him, same types who poured money into so-called "science" sending Novid and swift-mutating genetic weirdness worldwide–oh, sure, there had been show trials in the twenty years or so between Bloc Secession and the bombing of Fort Clinton kicking off civil war instead of uneasy "border actions," but everyone knew the only difference between a racketeer in the Bloc and one in Fedi-Mex was the size of the government contract.

Still, better the Feds and their lumbering bureaucratic bullshit than the midnight raids, the Black Beetles, the blaring loudspeakers, the camps. *Distarritz,* the dark-eyed bitch shivering behind her had said, and that wasn't a word civvies had any right knowing.

"Let's go," Coyote breathed, and at least Marge knew enough to do what a runner said after curfew. The streetlights were one off, one on; this shithole town was far enough from the front to have that luxury, but at any moment sirens could blare and canisters of whatever new bioweapon the fash had dreamt up could start drone-dropping.

Fuckers just never learned. Same shit, over and over, expecting different results.

The other shifter kept right on her shadow, which normally would've been irritating. But at least Marge didn't have to be hurried, and a half-hour later Coyote held a sheaf of rotting plasilka fence-net aside, sniffing delicately.

Her nose said nobody had come this way since last time; her junkyard sprawled under a cheese-yellow waning moon. To others, the jumble of dead ends between towers of stacked, rusting vehicles was a health hazard without even the value of scavenging since antifrik and sol-zaag had put paid to petroleum; the only reason it hadn't been plowed under and rezoned was the war.

Peace would be great, sure, but at least Coyote didn't have to find another place to live at the moment. She scuttled through the labyrinth, not bothering to double back or confuse the trail.

Anyone who came in here with bad intentions would get what they deserved.

Near the south edge of the yard–because only a dipshit would put themselves right in the middle–rusted, corrugated panels were bolted between rotting cargo trailers, forming a long, low building visibly reeking of neglect. Coyote muscled aside the guest entrance's cover, not bothering to wince at the screech of protesting hinges, and beckoned Marge in. "I'm not offering you a drink, so don't expect it."

"Fucking hell," Marge half-whispered. "This looks like a serial killer hideout, I don't expect a glass of milk."

Coyote snorted, almost against her will, but the noise was covered as she hauled the door shut. "Lights," she said, and hit the switch halfway through the word.

The other shifter didn't hiss, though her rapid blinking returned. She eyed the long strips of koreltube festooning the walls–a little juice and they glowed bright enough for all but the pickiest of detail work–and looped over the two bays dug out of oil-soaked sandy dirt, one empty, the other with a dangling chain-wrapped metal quadruped in its throat.

"There's your patient, doctor." Coyote pointed. "Full toolkit in those cabinets, and if something you need's not there, check the pegboard."

Marge's frown was very near thunderous, her long nose wrinkled. "What the hell is that?"

"You're the mechanic." Coyote ambled past the empty bay; a large white fridge, almost swallowed by the collection of junk serving as a wall, glowed pristine as a fresh implant in an otherwise toothless mouth. "Figure it out."

It took a certain type of person to mutter *oh honey what happened to you* while shoulder-deep in metallic DONQ-E42 guts, but apparently Marge fit the bill. Coyote perched atop the fridge, cross-legged, swigging from a condensation-dewed bottle rescued from the appliance's depths. Picking up a case of Hearne Lager from South Jupo on her last run–the Federated Mexico interior instead of across the battleline into what historians had christened the Neo-Texas Bloc and runners now called Lindyland–had been an inspired bit of thievery.

Well, maybe not stealing, since it was what she was owed. She'd brought the fingernail drive freighted with evidence to that poor dumbass soldier's parents so they could prove Private Jepstrom hadn't died from enemy fire at all, and maybe the court case was going their way now. Stopping to lift the beer–and a few other articles–from the soldiers trying to harass said family into dropping their inquiries could be considered a reasonable bonus.

What she'd done to them *after* taking both suds and underwear might not, though. A hazy, almost forgiving smile tilted Coyote's lips, exposing strong, crowded teeth.

The indifferently bolted stairs fastened to the side of the work bay trembled a bit as Marge climbed out, moving with swift assurance and ducking at just the right moment to avoid being brained. "All right, should be fine. Want me to switch 'er on?"

"Him," Coyote said softly. Then, a little louder, "Just stand back, I'll do it."

She hopped from the fridge's top, belched sonorously,

and strolled to the bay, setting the bottle down carefully on a stack of ammo crates. A tracer round in here and the entire place would go sky-high, but she slept better with supplies handy.

Besides, who wanted to live forever? Especially in this shitheap of a world.

The tab-tag was in her pocket; Coyote stepped close to Chicken's head. The DONQ-E unit was quadruped, long-nosed, and packed to its high narrow ears with marvels of anti-surveillance and other tech she'd paid to upgrade more than twice now. Entirely illegal and goddamn useful, the unit had been patched so many times there were probably no original parts left on him.

Should've named him Theseus. Coyote hit the tab. A flat metallic shine filled Chicken's oculars, which protruded almost as far as her own, albeit to either side instead of a predator's forward stare. Initial boot-up took only a few nanoseconds, and true to form the DONQ's head shot out on its long neck, gleaming oil-bathed teeth chomping shut with a sickening thud nearly three and a half centimeters from Coyote's midriff. *Fuck, I think this bitch made him faster.*

But fast as Chicken could get, someone else was still in charge. Coyote's fist flashed out, banging right above and between his eyes, and the solid sound of the blow reverberated through the entire jerry-rigged garage.

"Fucker," Coyote hissed. "*Behave*, or I'll jam sand up your assport."

Chicken's gyros and stabilizers cycled up. The sequence finished, and the DONQ's eyes flashed green. He didn't kick against the restraints but eyed Coyote balefully, ears up and his remote tab-tag vibrating in her hand. The tab's haptic pulse-pattern said all systems were operational, and the holo-readout hovering overhead returned the same information.

Chicken's hooves twitched, one after another, and the last holo-line turned beautiful emerald.

"Well," Coyote drawled. "Fuck fire and save matches. Marge, is it?"

"Yeah." The mechanic scrubbed at her hands with a scrap of nanocloth, though even the shift might not get those oil stains out. Looked like more of a nervous tic than actual cleanliness, but who didn't have a few of the former these days? "Lots of nonstandard stuff on that unit. I had to guess in a couple places, and I updated a few others. Should run nice and easy for at least three months, and when that's done..."

"Get yourself a beer from the fridge." Coyote shook her head, stuffing the tab back in her pocket. Chicken began secondary testing and a self-lube cycle, still staring murderously at his owner. "*One* beer. Come over to the table, lay out the money you've got, and tell me everything."

"You mean it? You'll take the job?" Marge clutched at the rag, blinking even harder. She had to know two hundred wasn't even enough for secondhand gear, let alone a trip over the border.

"I'm in," Coyote said grimly. "And I already know how I'm gonna run it, if you keep your fuckin head and do what I say. If you don't want the fuckin beer, though, that's up to you."

UNIVERSAL SYLLABLE

Drood's loaf-shaped silver trailer out past the city limits held a fug of yeast and rancid petro-lube; the man was always filthy as a runner in a shellhole. Downstairs on the first floor of the hollowed-out concrete shelter beneath, though, filtered air was sweetly cool and the crystalline fish tanks along one wall burbled happily, full of gem-bright cloned piscines.

The other side of the rectangle was taken up with a long gleaming counter, and metal racks behind it—or in the shelter's further depths—held whatever a runner might need. Given enough time and the proper inducement, he could get his hands on almost anything.

Especially since the failed second offensive back in Year Four of the war.

"Fucksake ya fucker, fuck the whafuck," Drood said, morosely. His right index finger was firmly up his nose, digging with sensuous care, but that didn't interfere with his ability to calculate a good return-on-investment or protest when he felt his personal margin was being unduly shaved.

"You moved all that nice cargo I brought back last month, stop bitching." Coyote tapped at a handheld tablet showing the bits of inventory Drood might be willing to part with. "You don't have any soffa grenades? What about through Gospher?"

"Fucking fuckhead." A slow roll of meaty shoulders, which did not interfere with his nasal prospecting. "Fucked with the fuckin em-pees."

Now that was news. Coyote cocked her shaggy, particolored head. "They must've found out about his flimsy forging; I told him to cut that shit out. Hey, size that bitch for a rig, will you?" She indicated Marge with a single flicker of her own bony shoulder.

"Fucking knows how to fuck 'em?"

"Even if she don't she can still *carry* a few irons."

"I know how to shoot," Marge said, softly, and turned away to study the fish tanks.

That was the great advantage of Drood's chosen language: it all depended on a single universal syllable. Some runners swore he quoted Shakespeare, Borges, and He-Tsing at home alone with a fifth of engine-tub rye, but Coyote thought it highly unlikely the man had ever picked up a book that didn't have holofilm titties bouncing inside.

"See?" Coyote's teeth were bared, and the expression could be mistaken for a cheerful smile. "And give me some fuckin soffs, I know you're holding."

Drood rubbed under his greasy mop of dark hair with his left hand, finally extracting the prize from his right nostril at the same moment. The man was a parallel-processing genius.

"Fuuuuck." He drew the word out. "Fuckin fuckers, half a fuckin duz."

"That's my boy." Coyote glanced at the total and hid a wince. But it was far, *far* more expensive to find out mid-run that you didn't have something your nose had tingled for when looking at a catalog.

Money was cheap. Continued existence with a modicum of comfort was... otherwise.

"Shit," she continued, her gaze snagging on an item. "You got the peanut butter bars now? You sonofabitch."

"Fuckin-A," Drood agreed, placidly. "Fuckin held the fucks, for fucksake."

Why, Drood, I didn't know you cared. "I'll take 'em." She swept the list into the tablet's outgoing basket icon, and let the piece of tech clatter onto the counter's shockproof surface. "Usual place, twelve hours. Any requests?"

"Fuckin Lindyfucks, fuck 'em up." Now the tall man's gaze was hot and direct, a coal seam burning underground. "Ten per."

That was low, but he knew she was good for an honest count, no scalps or other body parts required as proof. "Fifteen."

"Fuckin sold." He spat in his palm, she spat in hers, and his big warm paw, moist with saliva plus God alone knew what other secretions, nearly swallowed hers. "Fuckin frag 'em, dogbitch."

"You know it, you filthy motherfucker." She reclaimed her limb, turned on her heel, and set out for the stairs. "Come on, Marge. We're done here."

"Thank you very much," the civvie said primly, and Drood's reply was a polite enough obscenity. Marge cast a few longing looks over her shoulder at the tanks, but followed obediently enough.

Which was great... but Coyote didn't have a good feeling about this run. At all.

Sixteen hours later they were in the desert with Chicken.

CHUPACABRA NOVA

Plenty of ungifted thought prewar Lindy-funded biological experiments were responsible for the very existence of shifters, but there were stories about two-skins at least as old as humanity itself. When Margery Tasso had the luxury of thinking about it, though, she could allow that perhaps the Novid-A pathogen–with its fast mutations and hijacking of a previous coronavirus allowed to run rampant through the world's population since at least '19–might have kick-started a mutation process or two.

Others thought the plague had simply liberated shifters from secrecy, since they ended up immune from that particular pathogen. Novid had been meant to clear the globe so the big blond clones of a certain rich gank could inherit it all; the fact that the virus's descendants now ravaged seceded Lindyland far worse than Mexi-Federal, Cascadia, or Transcanadian territory was something approaching bleak irony. Other continents had their own problems, or were waiting to see how all this would shake out.

Marge liked history; it was a good way to see what was coming around to bite you now. However, she did *not* enjoy trudging around in the desert for days on end behind an illegally modified DONQ unit and a scrawny, morose shadow.

Guessing another shifter's second skin was pretty easy. If the smell didn't give it away, usually the movements did; only the ungifted had trouble figuring out the differences between modern sartorial oddity, augment surgery, cosmetic jacking-up, or a bona fide animal spirit choosing to share itself.

Of course, there were the shifters who wore what they were flagrantly in non-fash societies, either because they had a deathwish or thought themselves bulletproof against bigotry. Marge still hadn't decided which classification this scrawny, bug-eyed woman fell under.

Oh, sure, her shift was plainly visible, especially with that mop of particolored hair. Red, brown, black, a smattering of white and grey, all mixed together like an enthusiastic toddler had been in charge of the dye job and hacked into a mass as if the same kid had taken to it with blunt, petrol-powered landscaping tools–but that could've been a conscious choice.

It was only on closer examination that the ugly, disjointed face and restless twitching became a strangely harmonious whole instead of a collection of possibly radiation-mutated oddities all rolled into a half-cocked shift. There was clearly nothing wrong with the woman's control over her flesh, or the change granted by her other half.

And if you had any other doubts, rumor would clear up the riddle.

Can't help you, Fassby had said, pushing half the Federal credit chits back across the table. Then, as Margery stared with smarting eyes and claw-throbbing fingertips, he'd sighed and returned the other half, while the dust-choked ceiling fan in his "office" sent down an anemic draft doing nothing to cool the space. *Go out to the Mudhole after dark. Look for the skinniest, ugliest bitch there, and I don't mean maybe. Her name's Coyote, she's fuckin crazy.*

Of course Margery had checked it out, so far as she could. Everyone agreed on three things: Coyote was a runner, she took jobs nobody else would touch, and she was bugfuck.

So far, so good. But still, looking at the runner ambling along with apparent unconcern, a faded and nearly shapeless hat jammed over her hair–both hat and fur, Margery had to admit, were good camouflage for this slice of desert–and her patched jeans stiff with dust, a hip-length dun jacket with chewed-looking fringe swaying gently... well, it wasn't exactly awe-inspiring.

Dawn was a few hours past and heat shimmered over flat sand-choked nothingness. Margery hated sweating, and she hated glare. Most of all, she hated the dry breeze desiccating her sensitive nostrils, chapping her lips.

No, that was a lie. First place on her personal hate parade was reserved for the thought that Natandre was suffering and this strolling Coyote bitch wasn't hurrying at all. They were called *runners*, for fucksake, what was she doing walking for days? Impatience beat behind Margery's pulse, and she could have screamed with frustration.

They had to be near the border by now, moving parallel so far as Marge could tell, and several likely-looking arroyos or ravines had snaked northward, in the direction she guessed Lindyland lay. This country was so godforsaken there were no frontline troops, since holding it was more of a drain than simply sending drones over at intervals.

But the runner just kept plodding along, so–

Coyote froze between one step and the next. The DONQ unit did too, front left mechanical leg in midair, several heavy bags and cartons of gear piled on its reinforced back and its ears twitching like its owner's. In fact, Margery nearly ran into the quadruped's hindquarters, and swore under her breath.

"Shut the fuck up," the runner whispered, her lips barely moving, the words falling flat. "Stay here."

Before Marge could reply–if she'd wanted to, which she wasn't at all sure about–the other shifter dropped to all fours. The fringe on her dust-colored jacket blurred her outline as she skittered crabwise off to the right, plunging into a small ravine choked with what looked like dead sagebrush and sand-smothered boulders.

Oh, fuck. Only the fact that the DONQ unit stayed in place kept Marge from taking off in the opposite direction, suddenly sure she'd been lured out here to die.

It was easy to get killed for a paltry pile of chits, and nobody would miss her. Plus, she'd been honest with the runner, which might be a massive mistake. There were stories about entire convoys scavenged by unscrupulous guides, and every once in a while soldiers out on patrol came across shallow graves, those fleeing Lindyland's heavy-booted clones putting their faith in the wrong person, betrayed mid-journey. It was a crapshoot, but she had no choice, because Nat was all she had left and was counting on her big sister to do something, to save the day once more, so–

A soft, slithering noise. A crunch. The DONQ unit's ears focused forward and slightly to the left, quivering, and the contraption settled more solidly on its hooves, sinking a few millimeters into sandy earth.

They said the shaggy hide camouflage meant you didn't see mutated chupacabras novas–as opposed to the old pre-Lindy cryptids–until they were right on top of you, and it was true. The pony-sized predator burst from whirling sand, splattering caustic foam from snapping jaws, and leapt right *over* the DONQ. Marge's shift burned inside her bones; she staggered backward, hissing, claws bursting free and the certainty that she was about to be eviscerated forcing her into a defensive crouch.

Crunch. A dust-colored blur hit the thing hard, tumbling it sideways. The DONQ didn't move except for its swiveling ears; a howling, spitting, screeching knot of fur, teeth, claws, and fringe rolled, sending up a cloud of tiny particles. Violent white sunshine refracted, foam-stacked bubbles of the chupacabra's saliva pop-steaming against hardpan.

Another crunch, this one meatier and full of bonesnap. A knife-thin shadow rose in the heart of the dustcloud, and as flying bits of dirt settled Margery could pick out details–bladed nose, big blinking eyes, thin threads of steam as treated cloth repelled highly alkaline saliva, the fringe on Coyote's jacket twitch-swaying.

"Motherfucker," the runner said, calmly. "Marge? You still large and in charge over there?"

"F-fine." Margery's tongue felt too big for her mouth; her teeth had lengthened. She settled fully back into biped form, blinking, and wished the goddamn sun wasn't so bright.

Rain would be worse, though.

"I'm good," she repeated. "You hurt?"

"Not fuckin likely." The runner stretched, vertebrae cracking as they popped back into place. Quick twist of her head to one side, then the other, rolling her thin shoulders, then she bent to pick up her hat and jammed it back on. "If this bastard was carrying eggs we could have breakfast, but it's just as well. Wanna make the Skull before noon." A bright, pearly flash–her teeth, shown in a wide jackal grin. It was by far the happiest she'd looked since Marge met her. "You gotta piss, go over there. Sometimes cargo kidneys get a little unhappy after seeing a goatsucker."

Margery hated peeing al fresco, but her bladder was

indeed feeling a bit stretched. At least the runner had thought to pack a roll or two of Federal-issue surplus asswipe, which was somehow more surprising than the ease with which she'd killed one of the more dangerous mutations wandering around between Lindyland and Mex Federal.

They plodded on, but now Marge studied Coyote far more carefully.

Maybe being bugfuck had its good points.

WOLVES

The civvie shifter held up well, all things considering, and fell into the rhythm of travel with relative ease. They made good time that day and were sheltered in the Skull's jumble of rock, scrub, and a few water-trickle caves before the real heat hit. Plenty of critters were lured to the pile's relative coolness, even if drinking anything seeping from its stone was a good way to end up raving with worse thirst or just plain dead.

Marge's blinking became sporadic and stopped altogether as she studied the hole Coyote had chosen. She ran her fingertips over a vein of black stone running down the east wall, speckled with irregular blue and orange flecks, and tapped gently as if testing reflexes. "Oh, my," she whispered. "Good stuff here. Really good stuff."

Coyote snorted. "Don't get too attached." *You'll probably never see this place again.*

"Still. It would be nice to... Do you ever just bring people out here? I'd pay."

"Sure, take a nice restday hike past the chupas and other mutant shit, not to mention the snakes and putawasp towers, with Lindy drones overhead and..." Coyote frowned at the readout on her antique but highly updated handheld unit. "Just be quiet, for fucksake, I got work to do." They were close to the start line for the run itself.

"Can I help?"

"Sure you can. By shutting the fuck up." Going over the border wasn't like dodging curfew. If Chicken's blur field faltered, if they ran across a patrol and a stray shot took out a vital piece of gear, if weather conditions changed or something more dangerous than a stupid goatsucker or a sandworm got interested in trespassing bipeds—there were a hundred and one ways to get fucked in the wilderness, and exponentially more crossing a border overrun by trigger-happy Federals or insect-masked Lindy clones fresh off the processing line and jacked with combat implants, not to mention biological experiments run amok.

And that wasn't even counting what she was about to do once the plan really got going.

So Coyote triple-checked every piece of gear, kissing her left index knuckle occasionally for luck. She made sure the straps were tight, ran four overlapping diagnostics on Chicken's various hardware and subroutines, tested every knife in or under her clothes, and inspected the pistols strapped low on her skinny hips as well as the bandolier across her chest holding two soffas, just as she had that morning before setting out. Both rifles—hers and the one she'd have her cargo hold—got their own pre-crossing exams, passing with flying colors, and finally Coyote squatted easily at the cave mouth, staring into dayglare with slitted eyes, an illusory breeze patting her forehead since she'd pushed her hat back.

Don't brood on it. You knew sooner or later this would happen; every bitch has her day.

She chewed on a peanut butter Jvstin bar, enjoying the chalky taste as it cleaned her teeth, fragments settling in dental crevices. Her tongue would work those tiny bits free while she thought or waited.

Marge moved around the cave, stepping lightly and possibly enthusing inwardly over the walls. *Let her*, Coyote thought, and wasn't surprised by the other shifter's step suddenly turning soundless.

Yes, now she knew what Marge's second skin was. No wonder she dyed her hair; the question was, had she done it for cosmetic vanity, to make sure the pale stripe wouldn't show at night, or...

Coyote's head rose slightly. She sniffed, dragging the air deep, tasting.

Sand. Creosote. A porcupine had been past in the last twelve hours or so; a polecat had too. The dry oily funk of reptiles–there was a mojja-nest somewhere around here, but those were only interested in carrion and wouldn't come near a shifter until the corpse started to rot. Of more concern was the faint trace of shaggy fur, amber eyes, and a very familiar note of bitter almond.

Fuck. Well, if they moved fast enough, the pack might never know she was here. No use in worrying at the moment.

Coyote finished her protein bar, retreated into the cave's relative coolth, stretched out next to Chicken, and napped.

Hard diamond points glittered dryly overhead, the desert breathing as day's heat leached upward. Waning moon meant cobalt darkness, both hills and scrub dyed indigo; Coyote hurried her cargo down from the crest of a slight rise, uneasy at being silhouetted for even a moment.

Her nape was itching, a bad sign. Nothing had gone wrong

yet, which was another. And her pinkie fingers tingled, which could only mean one thing.

She halted, motioned to Marge. "Go over there." A half-mouthed whisper, a reasonably gentle shove in the right direction. "Ravine. Chicken will follow. Stay."

At least this cargo had learned not to ask stupid questions. The faint noises of Chicken pad-gliding instead of using his hooves couldn't be helped. Coyote crouched and waited, the deeper shadow of her hat brim ending just above her bared teeth.

The wolves melted out of the blue one by one, grinning, tongues lolling even when they shifted to biped. The largest gave a low happy growl, shaking his ruff, and the tang of bitter almonds became pronounced as his shoulders swelled.

"Evenin, Weimmar." Coyote's haunches were already tense, her fingertips dangling near sandy earth. Looked like a boy's night out, which was bad news indeed. "Don't you have roadkill to chew on?"

"Bad night for you, jackal-bitch." Weimmar's teeth snapped twice, *chik-chuk*, like pool balls on a hard, clean break. "Take your hair home to Matta, she'll be happy to hang it on our fence."

"You two finally get married?" Coyote didn't quite laugh, but it was damn close; Lukash's daughter could've done a lot better than this punk. "Or is she just letting you keep the bed warm until a real mate comes home from the front?"

He snarled, a low thrumming sound, and fuck's *sake* but it was so easy to provoke him. It wasn't even enjoyable, just something that had to be done.

The growl separated into words, but only barely. "Warned you to stay off our patch."

"Land don't belong to you, doggie-o. Not even if you piss on it." She'd have to lead them away from the cargo and

Chicken, lose them in a tangle of ravines about two klicks north, and double back. Which would tack too much time onto the run, but–

The rest of the wolves started slinking in, and now she had to bleed one in order to make the others angry enough to chase her. Coyote hunched, hands tingling as claws sprang free, hide rippling, individual hairs rising...

And a shadow bumble-streaked between two of the wolves, skidding to a dust-puffing stop while swelling upward. A clicking hiss turned into a low, chuffing snarl as a drift of bloodthirsty pungent near-musk exploded, almost drowning out the canine reek of Weimmar and his four good packbuddies.

"Wha*fuck*?" The wolf sounded genuinely startled. He skipped backward a full two paces, small pebbles grinding under bootheels. At least he wore decent footgear, even if the big rodeo belt buckle was enough to make an onlooker cringe with secondhand embarrassment.

"Back off." Marge's light contralto had deepened, turned husky, and her shoulders widened with packed muscle. The low grinding sound didn't fade, simply rose and fell with the words. "This one's *mine*, ya numbnuts, and I will bite your fucking muzzle off before I rip your spine out through your asshole if you take one step closer."

OVER THE BORDER

"Through his asshole." Coyote could not seem to stop grinning as she strolled, each easy swinging stride nonetheless moving them along at a good clip. She scanned the western horizon, checked the sky with a quick glance, and may even have stifled a chuckle. "Pretty good."

Marge's shuffling only looked ungainly; she was nowhere near breathless and made very little noise. "I just don't like bullies."

The familiar tingle of Chicken's blur field played over them both; no drones yet, but that could change in a hot heartbeat. Just after midnight a far rumble of artillery had lit up somewhere to the east—a simple local action, probably a feint or spoiling attack.

"There were only five," Coyote pointed out.

Marge didn't snort, but it was probably close. "Five against one."

"I could've asked them to go get a few of their friends to make it even." Coyote bounced on her forefeet for a few steps, springing along. "Don't worry," she continued, sensing Marge stiffening to look over her well-padded shoulder. "They don't come close to this part of the border. Just bad luck, them being on that slice of their range, and now maybe we won't have more."

Marge halted suddenly. Which meant Coyote and Chicken had to as well or the blur would be useless.

"This is a mistake." The cargo's voice shook slightly. "It's a stupid plan, I don't know why I agreed. You're going to get killed and my sister will still be locked up there. I can't–"

"Rabbiting." Coyote sniffed, deeply, and wished she could spit. A clot of phlegm spattering the sand might make a point. "It's about now that every cargo starts to get jumpy. Just ignore it, and do what I tell you."

"You're a real bitch, you know that?"

"So everyone says. Besides, we crossed the border a klick and a half ago, Marge-in-charge." Coyote's teeth gleamed, and under the hat's shadow her bulging eyes were hot coals. "We're in Lindyland now, so keep the fuck up."

She set off again, with that same deceptively lazy stride. Marge had to hurry, or be left behind.

PART TWO
THE CAMP

BETRAYAL DELIVERY

Two days later at sunset, a betrayal took place in a townlet on the outskirts of a war-flattened mass once named Odessa; the reclamation and rebuilding effort was "temporarily" paused due to conscripted labor urgently needed elsewhere. Still, the installation–possessing a highly classified name–lay astride several useful transport routes and was patrolled by clones in black uniforms, each precisely 1.92 meters tall and with only a 1.5 kg acceptable weight variation, their shining coal-colored bucket helmets fitted with insectile respirator masks whenever they ventured outdoors.

The front line was distressingly close, which meant Lindy clones outnumbered both regular soldiers and the support staff who wore respirators outside and often in, as well. Paradise was only for the pure, and damage from a stray viral mutation or bioweapon blowback was to be devoutly avoided–by those who could afford to do so.

At the east end of the pseudo-village lurked a two-story building painted deep green, its roof shimmering under a permanent blur field. Trim white-painted boxes full of blooming orange nasturtium sat under its barred windows, and uplifting choral music regularly blared from speakers mounted outside, providing aural camouflage as decreed by a subsection of Homeland Internal Security regulations.

Not that much noise ever escaped the basement, and those who were loaded into lumbering transports through the freight bays in back were largely sensa-hooded, incapable of screaming anyway. The offices on the second floor hummed so productively any stray agony drifting up staircases or down hallways was immediately, cheerfully ignored.

It wasn't unusual for someone to lug a body festooned with filament restraints up the three stairs to what was known as the service entrance. Nor was it unusual for a belching petroleo-era truck to wobble up, carrying a cargo of tagged and bagged undesirables, citizen or non.

Most unofficial drop-offs happened under cover of darkness, but there wasn't anything wrong with arriving a little early. Usually the fee was a certain number of ration chits per undesirable, more if a certain piece of freight's ident matched any number of lists known as Father's Specials. An additional benefit was the coveted green holo-stamp on a heavy plasteel card, theoretically allowing priority processing at checkpoints.

For such benefices, those who lived near the front kept a sharp eye out for any refugee, spy, or disliked neighbor. A certain amount of overflow from parts more interior was also processed in this locale, since it was along a major route for sending reinforcements to do their duty to the Bloc.

Willingly, or otherwise.

The "concerned noncitizen" making this delivery was herself an undesirable tainted with genetic sludge, but her card had the yellow seal which meant she was engaged upon

Special Duties and therefore untouchable for the moment. Trouble began when she insisted she had been promised a certain consideration in return for a particular cargo, though that was not entirely out of the ordinary either.

To build the shining new utopia, it was sometimes necessary to have the trash take itself out. Or denounce itself, as the case may be.

The woman wouldn't budge from before the desk until the duty officer called Upstairs, sending up a geneprint of the cargo as well. Whatever reply he received made the paperwork soldier stiffen, the sudden draining of blood from his face visible since his standard-issue "inside mask" was two nasal filters and a mouth shield. Like every Lindy clone he had slightly protuberant eyes, blinking furiously without the protection of a full respirator mask meant for outside use. The blue of said oculars was a few shades off standard, probably from a contaminated strand or two of protein matrix in his making; he would never achieve the highest echelons.

Even a slightly damaged clone was of higher status than the rest of the Bloc's supine population, though. After all, they were perfected copies of Father, who always knew best; consequently, the clone's mouthshield-muffled mumbling into an old-fashioned handset was properly submissive but not fawning.

Federal jamming and encryption-breaking of digital traffic was a perpetual risk, as was resistance hacking, so sensitive installations more often than not reverted to older tech.

"Yessir," he finished, and laid the handset down with the sour expression of any bureaucrat forced to relay unpalatable news to unwashed plebes. He eyed the dark-haired, heavyset woman standing before his desk; the undesirable at her feet was filthy with dust and limp inside its bonds. "Your family member's case is being reconsidered. If you were to bring in, say, a similar high-value target—"

"I was told." The woman's chin jutted; she didn't even wear a filtering mouthguard, but what could be expected from impures? Especially those so low as to turn on their own kind for a few more days of survival. "I was *promised* my sister would be—"

"You want to join her, and this piece of shit too?" The duty officer's nostrils quivered, a heroic feat considering the silvery indoor-use filters jammed in to screen their flow. His breath was sour with antiviral spray behind his mouthguard. "Because that can be arranged, I can absolutely get a commendation for sending another turd to the can. Take your fucking chits and get out."

He tossed the clattering rings, and they nearly landed on the undesirable. Which must have woken it up, because it started to struggle against the filaments and nearly kicked its betrayer, making muffled sounds through its crude fabric gag. It was an ugly thing, rolled in sandy dirt, and the duty officer gestured to the two privates on guard duty. "Prep this for transport, boys."

That did it. The trash-gene turncoat bent, scooping up the ration chits, and avoided looking at the trussed undesirable. The same sand clung to her boots, and the duty officer sighed at the tracks left as she scurried out.

The skinny undesirable was hefted between two Lindy grunts like a sack of contraband, but not carried downstairs— the next scheduled transport was in less than a half-hour, and no doubt they were glad for a little less work. Instead, they marched in lockstep down a concrete-floored hall to the holding tank, where the new arrival was stat-chained, filament-unwrapped, strip-searched, kicked a few times for form's sake, jammed into a coarse orange Detainment shift reminiscent of an old-timey hospital johnnie, rewrapped in filament, and unchained.

Then a sensa-hood was thrust over its head and it was propped in a wooden stall, for it was a very high-value capture indeed.

EPPIKSALLY

Twenty-four hours later, another glaring neon pink sunset was rapidly dying and a series of tinny chimes screeched from whirring speaker beads drifting six meters above the pavement or beaten-earth alleys of Distarritz. The locale had begun use as a transit camp fenced by razor wire; lo-frik tracks coming into the south end were still live, though the frequency of shipments had plummeted of late. The camp personnel dormitories were very nearly luxurious, for the work occurring there was lavishly funded. Even kep barriers had been added, curtains of pinkish energy shimmering between needle-posts to deter any escape from those foolish or lucky enough to wriggle through plain old electrified razor wire.

Of course the quonsets for the "patients" and "research subjects" were a good deal less comfortable, and their sides often quivered slightly as the creatures packed within struggled against filament restraints or cage doors.

The battle line was some distance away and research facilities unable to be moved with the manpower crunch after a decade of a war some called "civil," so the front entrance gate–every quonset hut turning its back on the aperture–was also live, accepting regular visits by shiny black stretch-transports. Equipped with antiviral filters and deeply cushioned seats, the stretches carried high-level Lindy functionaries visiting the zoo for budgetary and policy decisions, not to mention plain old titillation.

More often, shipments arrived by dusty, belching petroleo truck, hood and cloth canopy both daubed with desert camo patterns–far more efficient than sending half a dozen trash-gene undesirables by coal-fueled lo-frik, though sometimes after a City Cleansing an entire trainload could chug in along the tracks.

Shipments from Cleansings were much rarer now, since the punishment brigades at the front needed warm bodies to bolster the clones. Even noncitizens carrying a load of shame were forced to do their duty to Lindyland. Yet the Black Beetles still harvested individual undesirables at midnight or snatched them from the street in broad daylight, and those genetically tainted with amusing or possibly useful mutations were sought, caught, shipped, and made to serve whatever bigotry-blinkered version of science fanatics play at.

The chiming of arrival set off a flurry of activity. Guards raced for the intake square, squinting against westering sunshine, their big black insectile masks hurriedly but thoroughly fitted. By the time a single wallowing truck between two bristling counterinsurgency humvells cleared the gate, processing was prepped and the cargo unloaded–a mere seven hooded bodies, all cocooned in filament, six with tags of varying colors denoting certain political, sexual, economic, or antisocial tendencies plus a secondary tag meaning trash-gene mutations of one type or another. The last one bore a single fluttering black tab meaning "dangerous/enhanced," and all were ready to be loaded onto single-celled hovergurneys.

Undesirables in other camps were herded on foot up scanning ramps, separated by gender, age, fitness, genetic rarity, P-factor, and last of all, harvestability. This couldn't be done with many trash-genes or enhanced undesirables; most were simply too strong and fast. Even a full squad of cloned soldiers with combat augments would have trouble with a single shifter, and barely mutated trash-genes often burned through sedation far too quickly for research staff's comfort.

The appearance of a tall figure, fully masked with mirrored visor and wearing a pristine white lab coat despite the dust, sent a buzz through the intake staff. Dr. Deranian rarely braved summer weather; the incoming material must be something special. Handheld units buzzed and processing was completed in record time, crisp salutes given with theatrical flourishes and the transport team, drivers and guards both, ushered toward the staff cafeteria for ersatz ration–and the chance of some gossip.

Most of the gurneys were bound for the medium-security Hepakah or Naduce quonsets. One, and only one, was bound for Eppiksally, rifles trained on the filament-bound figure every step of the way. Which either meant a specimen of great interest, or more than moderate flight risk.

Rumor had it the last big personnel change at Distarritz had been a real Cleansing in its own right, because a high-value undesirable had managed to abscond. Safer not to ask, and in any case nobody knew for sure.

Except Dr. Deranian, that was. He followed the single hovergurney and its black-tagged load to Eppiksally as dusk swallowed the camp, staying far enough back that the static-charged dust didn't foul his white coat.

At least, not much.

A sensa-hood was meant to disorient, especially sensitive shifter noses, ears, eyes, tongues. There were tricks to ameliorate the worst effects–Coyote knew them all–but it was still painful as fuck. Federal standard doses of bamzedrine helped, *if* you didn't have a metabolism jacked up high enough to burn off both the 'drine and sedation.

Sure, you could take a massive dual jolt, but 'drine had the side effect of emptying the large intestine in explosive fashion. Protein bars had a fifty-fifty chance of bricking up the works enough to avoid that particular embarrassment, though most runners with the shift didn't take those constipatory odds. If caught, they'd deal with the distortion, nausea, and feedback whines *au naturel*.

Given what else awaited them in that situation, it could almost be called bravery.

The biggest trick was mental, and an old friend. Disassociating enough to be almost halfway into the shift, a peculiar state of fierce, half-relaxed concentration often used while loping through the desert at night, every hair quivering and every muscle fully aware. At the same time, the body had to stay inert in pink biped form, rolling with punches, slaps, and kicks like a sack of wet meat while a tiny motionless speck buried between solar plexus and belly button counted off steps, tracked the slight jarring rumble of transport wheels or glide over roads, recited an inward *one-two-three*, waltz time, in the sickmaking rock-a-bye of a hovergurney.

There was always the risk of miscounting, of slipping. But she was fairly confident her plan had held up, and when the hood was ripped from her head and the violent hyperassault of ordinary sensation swamped her, Coyote promptly turned her head and heaved as if terrified and disoriented.

Harsh orangish korel light. Thick fog of disinfectant, effluvia, pain, and old blood. Metal clanging. The filaments didn't loosen until the shelf was rolled feet-first into the cage bay and rotated vertically, at which point a mild Sebastol current ran through the whole thing and the cruel spidersilk strands went slack, pooling and retracting like unwrapping a ration pastry.

Coyote's pupils contracted, quick as a slamming door. Her nose ran, sour iron sludge at the back of her throat. She retch-sneezed, almost managing to splatter a white lab coat with sputum through the cage door's grillwork.

He made a small clicking noise behind his mask, tongue against teeth, hatefully familiar. Then came the dry, precise, fussily educated baritone, rendered nasal by filters clamped in his nostrils.

"Patient 713-KYT, how nice to see you again. Did you enjoy your time outside?"

You have no idea. Coyote kept hacking and spitting. If the desert hadn't dried her out, she might even have pissed herself just to add to the fun. Her ears throbbed–heartbeats, respiration, whine of live cage doors, the low constant scrape of dust-laden wind against curved prefab walls.

He suspected she was putting on a show–either that, or Deranian was eager for vengeance. He toggled the much stronger electric zap, and the entire cage became a live wire. Seizure raced through Coyote's muscles, bones creaking under merciless torque. She went ahead and screamed, a long, high yowl letting everyone know the bitch was back in town.

Not that any of her fellow inmates had been here long

enough to remember her first tenure; the good doctor tended to go through material fairly quickly. She couldn't even be sure her cargo-to-collect was still alive.

Finally the current shut off. Coyote sagged against one side of the openwork metal rectangle, forced to stay upright, not enough room to turn around or sit down. A little bit of leaning was the only rest allowed; compliance might earn a bigger cage in one of the other high-security quonsets.

Her heart hammered, lungs working in great heaving rasps.

Deranian leaned close to the door. This time she didn't try to spit, just dragged in what air she could reach even if it was tainted by his fucking cologne–Lindy Leather, because he was a true believer, and rewarded like one.

"Welcome home," Deranian whispered. "We're going to have quite a bit of fun, KYT. I've missed you."

Feeling ain't mutual, asshole. But Coyote let her eyes roll back, let her entire body sag as if barely conscious. Her shift knew how to play dead.

Finally, he turned and strode away, gesturing peremptorily at the guards and intake crew. Coyote strained her ears. The door slammed, and a silent, collective sigh of relief went through the sparsely occupied cages.

She waited. If anyone was going to whisper, now was the time.

Nothing. Of course, the Eppiksally security feeds were live and manned except for a few moments during shift change or while a drone bombing necessitated switching everything over to generators; plus, the cage-seals were high-priority and full of mechanical failsafes. Looked like they'd made a few improvements since her last stay.

Coyote let her breathing even out, let her pulse drop.

Hopefully Marge was large and in charge where she should be instead of getting any rabbit-ideas.

So far, everything was going according to plan.

FRESH MEAT

To save a few bureaucratic pennies, the korel glow switched off at midnight and the inside cameras popped over to infrared. Slight ripples of movement were audible throughout Eppiksally, though only to sensitive shifter ears. It was possible to relieve some of the agony of cramped motionlessness, *if* you were careful and slow.

Of course, if a sadist among the guards was looking for promotion there might be a snap inspection or a few random sessions of zap. You could never tell when they might get tired of playing with the non-shift undesirables and long for different fare.

Coyote's eyelids lingered at half-mast, bruises shrinking. Heightened healing meant faster metabolism, and though she'd taken down all the protein bars she could manage the timeline was still short. Her fingertips twitched, stretched, and began to pat at grillwork and bars.

Now the whispers began.

"Korinna." The first was from Coyote's right, a few cages away. "From Laredo."

"Abel." Another, closer to the door. "Idaho City. Real shithole, by the way."

A wheezing, tubercular cough came from the corner. "For fucksake, let me sleep."

"That's Joe," Korinna whispered. "He's from New Humboldt, they're not too polite there."

How sweet, introducing themselves to the new arrival. A real camp greeting. The strange part was that there were so few; last time, the cages had been jam-packed. A staticky hush descended, waiting for Coyote to add her own name.

When she didn't, Korinna spoke again. Clearly she held some kind of moral authority. Which would normally get her quickly decommissioned; in Eppiksally there was no prisoner promoted to q-cap, since there wasn't really a need to play divide-and-conquer.

Everyone was in a separate cage, and nobody expected to survive despite the gentle fiction of memorizing monikers, the vain hope of somehow passing on information to loved ones.

"It's all right." Her whisper was surprisingly gentle. "Tell us your name, so we can remember. So if someone—"

You idiot. "I'm just passing through." After the whispers, Coyote's tone—just a shade under normal speaking voice—was nearly a slap in the face.

"Well good for *you*," Joe hissed. "Mics are still live, so pipe down."

Coyote could have asked why they fucking asked questions if he wanted her to pipe down, but it didn't seem funny as it usually would. Besides, she was busy.

One claw-tip lengthened as she felt around the lock mechanism. They'd updated the design since her time, of course, but if she knew one thing about the fash it was that they didn't prioritize creativity. Fanaticism or bigotry killed any kind of true innovation, though both liked to steal everything possible and claim they'd invented it.

Plus the Lindy clones, like all mass-produced copies, were prone to both deviance and blurring, neither of which provided much fuel for imagination unless it was in the area of torturing the helpless.

More whispers raced through the quonset; Coyote didn't listen. She fingered the lock mechanism, brushed the cage door, tested the sides–careful to keep her movements within the visual tolerances of infrared blobs on watched screens. Her toes spread, gripping, and she tested the cage floor, openwork mesh to let effluvia drip through.

The lock was stubborn. She hadn't expected much else; getting a faulty one last time was a lottery-winning chance. Still, it would've been nice.

She leaned this way and that, testing the cage supports as well. Nice and stable. But the movement attracted their attention.

"Don't," Korinna whispered. "There's no way, and it'll just make trouble."

"What is she…" Joe was a curious curmudgeon, for sure. "Oh, fucksake. I hate new meat. Making me hungry."

"Shh." Abel, near the door. "Boots."

Silence fell, sharp and thick. The guard patrol ended up simply passing by; it wasn't a bunch of assholes looking to do a "spot check" or engage in a little recreational torture.

Finally Joe relaxed. "Can't hear 'em," he whispered, and the tiny voices resumed.

Coyote chose that moment to speak. "Natandre." Not quite a whisper, but not nearly so loud as she's spoken before. "Mid-twenties, from Old Houston. Heard she was here."

A brief, surprised quiet full of subliminal machinery-hum.

Finally, Korinna drew in a sharp breath. "Natandre. I think she's one of Dr. Death's favorites."

Bad news. Marge's sister stood a good chance of being dead by now, or worse. "He still working in Nekksandra?"

"The fuck," Joe nearly forgot to whisper. "She's a plant. Sull up, everyone."

Dumbasses. But you could never be too sure, in a camp. To betray another for an extra ration, for a shred of blanket, for the chance of another day breathing was a good tactic. Nobody could judge what you did in hell; you were already dead but the body didn't know it and grasped for continued existence with every possible means.

"Whatever," Coyote said, softly. "Keep going, I don't fucking care."

Time passed, the interior of Eppiksally a black well. Eventually, the inhabitants of this particular underworld continued their soft congress, pointedly excluding her.

In the darkness, Coyote kept working. There was no weakness to exploit in the cage, but there was nothing else to do. She expected to be dragged out at dawn, since Deranian would be eager.

She was right.

DOCTOR DEATH

Even through the sensa-hood, counting steps and feeling the hum of the hovergurney, Coyote could sense the general direction and distance. Dr. Death was indeed still working in the quonset christened Nekksandra.

Creature of habit. Well, weren't they all?

It was just the same—hefted with a jerk onto a cold metal slab, filament tightening cruelly, the hood ripped free to bludgeon her with a glare of white light and sudden, overwhelming sting-stink of antiseptic. Sure, transport staff had to playact at some professionalism, but no few of them enjoyed the flinch when a research subject found themselves on the slab with spiderleg armatures arching above, poised to jab, to cut, to cauterize.

"Well, well." Deranian did not quite smack his thin lips with anticipation; the smear representing him took on details as her pupils shrank and visual input cleared up. "Good morning, 713-KYT. It's been too long."

"You got it wrong, doc." Coyote's throat was desert-dry; no tube feeding this morning. "I'm not 713-KYT. I'm only three and a half." Of course they wouldn't get the joke; pre-Bloc media was ruthlessly censored and had been for at least three decades.

The tech hovering at the other side of the slab visibly swallowed, his Adam's apple bobbing. "Should I gag her, Doctor?"

Kid even looked a bit greenish. Must've been a new transfer; maybe Lindyland was finally scraping the bottom of their manpower barrel.

That was a vain hope. Others might argue the Lindys were about to crumble at any second, as the blockades continued to tighten and rationing bit, the repressive fist squeezed, the casualties mounted. Wishful thinking, according to one particular shifter bitch. After all, they had a bottomless well of the thing that counted.

Hate.

"No, thank you." Deranian's eyes had narrowed, but his tone didn't alter–dry, almost avuncular. He lifted something from the tray of sterilized tools to his right. A gleaming scalpel, but that didn't mean anything. Just theatrics, starting the mind games early to season the meat. "This one rarely cries out. Quite an interesting case; it seems to like pain. And sometimes it's even rather amusing. One might almost suspect higher-order thinking despite the contamination."

"I've..." The tech swallowed again. "The gene profile is very odd, sir, even for a mutant. What... what animal..."

"Robust little scavenger." Deranian laid aside the scalpel, selected something else. A high metallic drilling whine halted; it had been part of the soundscape since the hood came off, so the cessation was almost shocking. Muffled snorting could be heard–someone else had been held overnight for "observation" and was now getting the business from one of Doc Death's underlings.

Tests, they called it. No good grades, no passing, and nothing was learned. There was only excruciation.

Coyote's nose twitched, untangling scent-threads. Deep breaths, as if she were bracing herself for the experiments. Deranian lifted a syringe with a finger-long needle, displaying it clearly before setting it aside.

Four shifters including her own sweet self, all putting out waves of high stress and pain. Each held a tinge of Eppiksally's particular reek, good to know. Two were bleeding, red copper scraping against her palate. The sobber petered out, probably into unconsciousness. If the others were awake, they might be glad someone else had shown up to distract the damn "doctor."

"Fuckin poser," Coyote said, clear and distinct. "You got your medical license with ring tabs off Wordy beer cans. Send in ten, get a gimcrack; send in thirty, get a camp promotion."

The tech sucked in a breath, his eyes widening. Coyote smelled fermentation on him, a bright, hard note of cheap rationed distillation impersonating whiskey.

Deranian lifted something else. It was a bone saw polished to mirrorsheen, its triangular teeth glistening with disinfectant. "You see?" he said, still almost gently. "Almost, *almost* higher-order. If we can unlock this one, cure the regressive genetic tendencies while keeping the healing factor, well. Sky's the limit, Jenkyns."

But those soulless eyes of his had narrowed slightly.

She'd pissed him off. Coyote could mark it as an achievement; the bad ol' doc was famous for never raising his voice or hurrying. His sadism was the cold, methodical variety. Which probably helped when it came to getting funding from Lindbergh's toadies or the Father himself, a blubber-pile still propped up by those "immortality treatments" fash propaganda was always on about.

Now she knew the name of Deranian's tech, a small victory. Plus, the longer she dragged this out, the more time she had to sniff. One of the shifters had an odd tang to their scent—a familiar thread of rich black dirt and dark hair, calling up images of a pale stripe stubbornly refusing dye.

She had to be sure. Couldn't risk just imagining.

"My little failure." Deranian reached up to adjust one of the lamps, aiming the glare more securely into Coyote's eyes. "Don't worry. We'll cure you yet."

Looked like he'd settled on the saw. There was no bracing herself for what was about to happen, so she didn't even try. Well, not much.

Her body had other ideas, and strained against the filaments. The bonds would tighten right before he began to cut, unless he changed his mind mid-procedure.

The tech had several bottles of substances to rub into the wounds, too.

NEW DEVELOPMENT

Time always stood still in Nekksandra, but eventually, even Deranian grew fatigued. Hooded and gurneyed, Coyote counted steps and gauged direction again–yep, back to Eppiksally. But she'd heard the others get tied and bagged before her, so despite the decline in population, the greater camp schedule still held–four days on, half-day off, and during the latter, regular gene-trash undesirables were still on work duty outside.

Deranian's specials, however, weren't held for observation but tube-fed and sluiced on the half-days. For that, they had to be back in their cages. If one gave out overnight from the aftereffects of the doc's attentions, they were carted away for final processing–and harvesting–just after dawn.

Plenty of time. Or so she hoped.

Coming back into her body was fucking awful. The ol' doc had outdone himself, and she was a mess. Her remaining eye was at half-mast, he'd taken four teeth, broken a few more, her left hand was mangled by one of the chewing contraptions—with all that and what he'd done to her toes, the rest of the slices, abrasions, and chemical burns hardly mattered. The injections of biological agents were concerning—there was a chance, however minute, of something that could interfere with the shift.

Not paid enough for this. A grim laugh threatened to jolt its way free, but that might irritate the transport staff and would certainly trigger a tightening in the filaments. This was the bad part—no extra calories for healing, though she'd loaded up before beginning this section of the run.

Her cage clanged shut, the transport dicks trooping out in a hurry, ready for dinner and whatever form of liquid intoxicant could be brewed or found.

A muffled chorus of moans rose from the other three guests of Nekksandra. There was a rattle—maybe someone with the tail end of a seizure, maybe an attempt to alleviate fierce cage-cramps.

"Bob?" Korinna whispered. "Helga? Nat?"

"New meat's got moxie," a husky female voice answered, barely mouthing the words. "Trash-talked big D. Prolly still bleeding."

Of course I'm still bleeding. He'll do worse tomorrow, if he can. Coyote focused on her own pulse, high and hard. Too much adrenaline and cortisol in the stream, her shift unable to come down from fight-or-flight. Nowhere to run to, baby, nowhere to hide.

Normally she wasn't big on classical music, but that one was a good old corrida.

Coyote hissed through a few breaths, waiting to see if the lights flickered or a guard showed up. More hushed conversation, kept just below the threshold of even the most sensitive Lindyland mic. Finally, the silent third shifter from Nekksandra coughed, a deep racking sound.

"Fuuuuck," she whispered. "Kori? Joe?"

Real chummy in here. At least until the guards—or Deranian—figured out Korinna was holding her fellow prisoners together. Anyone capable of gaining respect or loyalty under these conditions was a threat to be taken seriously, nipped in the bud.

"Hey, Nat," someone whispered.

Fuck me, at last. Added to the scent, it had to be Coyote's target.

The lid of her remaining eye flicked open. Cage doors, walls spattered with desert dust and trails of dried filth, the floor of easily hosed-down lino—in the regular huts, it was packed dirt. Maybe some of the non-shifter undesirables even envied the fabled "better conditions" of Eppiksally, or the imaginary better rations and "medical care."

At least her right hand was intact—bruised and abraded, but no tendons severed. Coyote flexed fingers, thumb, and wrist, careful to keep the motion hidden from mounted fisheye lenses. Whoever was watching the cameras probably had a wandering gaze, anticipating half-day duties, but better safe than sorry.

"Natandre?" This time, Coyote whispered below the mic threshold as well. "Puerto Razon Middle School? Sennarita Gampin, third grade?"

Give me something only she would recognize, she'd said. Marge had thought it over, pursing her full, sculpted lips, and finally came up with the name.

She loved that teacher. It was Miss G says this, Miss G says that, all the blessed day.

Mechanical, humming silence filled Eppiksally to the brim. Even Korinna held her breath.

Finally, Nat responded. "Margie?" A tiny, threadlike sound.

"Whafuck?" Joe didn't think much of this new development, but it was Korinna who had the most presence of mind.

"Be careful, Nat. That one's new."

"Smells bad," Abel added.

You don't smell like no fuckin spring mornin yourself, sugar babe. Coyote's cracked lips pulled back, cooler air rasping over the exposed nerves of broken teeth sending little twinges down her neck. There was more conversation– Korinna cautioning, Joe attempting to provoke, Natandre nearly going above the mic threshold to get a response from the new meat.

Coyote said nothing else, focusing on her right hand. The shift wanted healing first, but she couldn't let it.

What she needed now were claws.

By the time midnight rolled around she was ready.

Holding the shift only in her cramped right hand wasn't the most difficult thing she'd ever done, but Coyote still sweated a little as she sawed at the bloody flesh below her right hip, down the groove between quadriceps and iliotibial band. Not a lot of nerve endings in that big ribbon of tendon, and she didn't think Deranian would start with taking the leg off that high up to see if it could regrow–but you never could tell, fucker was crazy.

Hopefully not crazy as Coyote herself, though.

The koreltube lights died right on schedule, cameras switching over to infrared. Coyote exhaled softly, dragging the sharpest claw on her right hand down the outside of her thigh. A little more digging, the pain nearly sweet because it was her own doing instead of administered while she was strapped down, and the razor tip–more sensitive than any

Lindy scientist would think, pressure exquisitely calibrated–found what it was looking for.

The best place to hide something was where nobody would bother looking. They did cavity searches, sure–but a long slim piece of metal buried in muscle fiber was something else, passing even through gora or magwave scans. A hot, thickening trickle of blood slid down her leg, drops landing in the waste pan underneath the cage floor.

Plink. Plink.

"That's fresh." Korinna whispered. "Who's bleeding? Sound off, everyone."

Coyote didn't bother. She drew the metal out, her remaining eye rolling and blinking fiercely. A wet, fiery finger traced down her filthy cheek.

I'm not fucking crying. It's just a reaction.

One down, one to go. Her fingers plunged back into the wound, denying its urge to close, to seal. Walking with this shit buried in her leg was fucking unlivable.

Good thing she'd been mostly carried here.

Once she had both small, thin implements free, she let out a not-quite sigh. A furious tide of whispers spilled through the interior of Eppiksally, almost triggering the mics.

Finally, the other shifters could sense something happening.

TIME TO MOVE

She'd expected the updated cage lock to be far more troublesome, and nearly fucked the entire run when it yielded to mere mild poking. Her infrared profile wouldn't change much with the movements, even if she had to lose some skin pushing a hand through the door's lattice, but breaking the live lock-circuit would cause all sorts of fun.

And she didn't want that just yet.

"The fuck are you doing?" Joe was having what might be called a fit. "Kori? What's the new meat doing? We're gonna get raided, fa fucksake."

Shut up, rabbit. There was one in every quonset, sometimes more. Monomaniacal focus on playing by the rules to survive might work for a while, but that was a rigged game.

Like everything else, especially in fash Lindyland. Bucking odds was a matter of timing. She'd lose sooner or later, sure; Coyote just didn't want it to be today.

The worst luck would be a snap inspection, which wasn't likely the midnight before a half-day. Of course, *sometimes* they happened, especially if a camp commander had a bug up their ass or been yelled at by higher-ups lately.

Just knowing the door was potentially dealt with was also a trap, because it might make her sloppy or provoke movement before go-time. There could also be a security measure or two added since her previous visit, ready to trip her up. Her prior escape had been a fluke and she was fucking insane to return, especially for a stranger, a measly few hundred credits, and questionable mechanic support to a nasty-tempered DONQ unit.

Why had she agreed? Partly because of pride, since she took jobs nobody else would or could. Partly because of Marge's blinking eyes, the little tics saying she'd grown up in the Bloc—like twitching whenever a *dear Leader* or *bless it* should be added to conversation, like slapping her hands flat on a grimy Mudhole table in the particular way schoolchildren were taught to when a teacher or other authority figure barked.

But most of it, Coyote had to admit, was personal. Unfinished business, she could say if asked, if she felt like answering at all.

Some part of this was just fucking ironic. Decades of the fash using Novid and other, far less wholesome weapons to wipe out everyone who wasn't a clone of Lindbergh *or* "certified pure"; it was darkly hilarious that shifters were visibly immune. The real joke was that the next step in evolution was staring fash fucks right in the face and they were still sticking with their little fantasies of a time that never existed, genetic heritages they couldn't claim.

Pure, her shaggy particolored *ass*. Only thing deserving that title was triple-distilled hooch.

Since she wasn't moving, Joe shut up. Thick silence filled Eppiksally to the brim. Coyote waited, and waited.

Surprisingly, someone spoke instead of trying to grab some sleep while the infrared was on. "Hey." A tentative little whisper. "Hey, new meat."

Coyote nearly rolled her eyes, but most of her concentration was now on holding the door-lock in the proper position so the circuit didn't break. Anything left over was shoveled into healing; *now* she could let flesh seal, bone slivers twitch back into place, hematomas reabsorb.

But slowly. So slowly, because she'd used up the bulk of her body's reserves staving off the process. It figured. A lot of shifters didn't bother with that kind of stubborn control, didn't practice it until too late, stayed sloppy because the ungifted were, after all, so slow and clumsy, so easy to deal with.

"New meat," Nat persisted. "You got a name?"

I'm just passin through. But Coyote made a soft, under-the-mic noise, almost a grunt.

"Margie." Nat slowed the name down, enunciated very clearly. "How do you know her?"

She got over the border and scraped together what she could to get you out, too. Made her case to the craziest bitch in Fed-Mexi, who was just dumb enough to take the job. Hope you're worth it, kid.

Marge clearly didn't know when to quit. She'd kept digging until she found a runner crackers enough to take on this job. Even if it was a double- or triple-cross, someone had to admire the flat-out moxie on the stripe-headed zaftig, and that one-eyed someone was holding a cage door shut with her unmutilated hand at the moment.

So, there it was.

A tiny tingle spilled down Coyote's back. One thing was for damn sure, the guard schedule hadn't changed since her time at Distarritz. The rhythm of the place was still etched into her bones.

It was shift change.

Time to move.

The combined infra-viz fisheye lenses were easy to spot, arranged along a few axes for efficiency and cost-saving because fash were nothing if not cheap as possible. Ideally both guards would be watching in the booth while one sat down and the other prepared to get the fuck off duty, but even clones weren't perfect *every* time.

Of course there was always the risk of some spit-shiny new jackass on deck, but certain risks had to be run. The cage door slid aside and rebounded with a rattling clatter, probably causing a squeal of feedback on the microphones. Automatic buffering would filter part of the sound, but any listener's headphones were most likely laid aside for the moment.

There was a time to lie in wait, curled nose-to-tail, and there was a time to burst into frenetic activity.

One-handed, she still managed to climb; Coyote was atop the row of cages in a few swift movements. Squeeze-slithering close to the wall where the infra and visible didn't catch, her shoulder whispering against the outer curve, she reached her first goal in a blurring cockroach scuttle almost before the cage had reclosed.

A yank on a lens housing loosened it enough to show fiberoptic cable behind. A quick claw-twist, a single bright blue-white spark, and that fisheye was dead in both visible and infrared. That took care of the quonset's opposite side; she kept going, the noise of knees and both hands slapping cage-tops might or might not break mic threshold. She ignored the bursts of agony flashing up her left arm. With any luck the cage door's circuit had resealed within the number of seconds necessary to turn its light back at the guard-shed to green instead of the yellow of *possible problem, oughta check it*; if she was given still more good fortune the lens she'd just disabled would be attributed to a local power surge.

While Deranian had been cutting and grinding, two of his happy little helpers had been conversing in low tones about the main 'lectric supply becoming intermittent at night, leading to micro-outages too short for the gennies to be switched over.

It was ridiculous, but a core article of Lindberghian faith centered on coal and petrol instead of cheap, effective solzaag, wind, or geothermal; even if it hadn't, the blockades meant trouble importing battery material. But they still rumbled along, putting up a fight; no, they weren't innovative or even particularly smart.

Just brutal, which overcame a lot of fancy thinking so far as Coyote could tell.

Hopping over the quonset's doorway had to be accomplished as silently as possible, and whispers raced through the cages. Korinna, of course, was quickest to figure out what the fuck.

"What are you doing?" she hissed, almost forgetting to keep it quiet.

"Son of a–" Joe didn't get the rest out before he was shushed. Someone moved in their cage, a metallic rattle covering the noise of Coyote's scrambling.

She found the housing she wanted–home to repeater and small processor. Loosened it with a quick yank, feeling around inside for a hex connector. If she could loosen it enough...

Look at that. A wild cackle rose behind Coyote's

breastbone; she denied the noise, swallowing a slightly acidic, blood-tinged burp. The fucking thing was loose anyway and had probably been randomly cutting out for an undetermined period.

Once you started poking past the façade, the vast shoddiness of the Bloc's "towering" achievements was revealed. Still, she was careful, loosening the hex a quarter-turn, no more, then slicing the main audio line with excruciating care. Her fingertips tingled, sensing the flow of electrons... then they didn't. It wasn't quite imagination; shifter senses were acute, and encompassed far more than those of the soft pink bipeds who thought themselves the natural owners of the world.

None of that mattered. What *did* matter was the breathing room incompetence and substandard infrastructure could give a wild creature intent on escape.

Coyote landed in front of Nat's cage. A quick sniff–oily dark fur bearing a pale stripe, blood and pain teasing at the predator spot on a shifter's palate, a faint androgen-tinged echo of Marge's solid hips and wide strong shoulders–verified the contents, and she rescued the two sharp pieces of metal she'd knotted into her camp smock. A mostly imaginary breeze caressed her bare legs, the promise of cooler air outside the stifling shed.

"Margie sent me," she confirmed, softly. "Bitch loves her baby sister, gotta admit."

"How... What..." Even through the cage door, Nat's confusion was evident.

"I'm leaving. You're cargo." Coyote knelt, and began working on the lock. It would go faster with both hands, even if one was a pulped mess, and if she got the doors open-and-shut fast enough they might have a chance. "Anyone else who wants to come along, speak up now or forever hold." *If you start yelling once we're outside the hut, I'll kill you.*

She didn't add the last part. Let it be a surprise.

PART THREE
THE TRICK

DARK POCKET

Hot white beams stabbed the desert night, glaring through veils of lifted dust, crawling along Distarritz's interior, the packed-dirt avenues and main concourse. The bars of searchlight sweeping outside the fences–both electrified razor wire and kep–moved a little more swiftly, though the guards watching atop evenly spaced towers were probably bored out of their tiny little clone minds.

After all, there was nothing but desert in every direction, a dusty rock-studded hunting ground for drones both Bloc and Federal as well as wild animals and the specter of thirst. Anyone insane enough to try escape was probably in a state of desperate stupidity as well–a point Joe had made twice before Korinna told him, in a fierce whisper, to get back in his fucking cage if he loved it so much.

Coyote almost liked the woman on the strength of that one sentence alone.

Move fast, freeze when I do. Don't make a sound and I'll take you to the wire. Once we're outside the kep I don't fucking care where you go but before then, try not to leave a blood trail.

Which pretty much covered everything, so far as she was concerned. Any asshole unlucky enough to be a Distarritz resident for more than a day could figure out the rest.

For all his bitching, Joe didn't want to be left behind. Korinna took rearguard, which was fine. No lock on Eppiksally's front door, because everything inside was caged and besides, who would be dumb enough for what she was about to do? Coyote plunged into a desert night, a piercing chill after the heavy, sweating confines of cage and quonset; every shifter in the group was packed in a sliver of shadow along the hut's side just in time.

Count. One, two, three...

She timed the sweep of lights, waiting until the pattern repeated despite the ragged breathing and subtle movement behind her, the saturating cloud of fearsweat more acrid than anything an ungifted could produce. Temps plunged in the dark hours; the desert was utterly democratic, you had the choice of dying from hypothermia or heatstroke, depending.

The cargo behind her shivered, pressing close enough to share a bit of body warmth. Natandre was taller than her sister, gaunt though with a certain breadth of shoulder. Her nose twitched just like her sibling's, and if they were caught in the lights she'd probably blink just like Marge, too.

Don't think about that. It was time to run instead of chew. Coyote hunched, tensing, and a ripple ran down the line. Her scent had changed, glands opening slightly–good as a shout to shifter senses.

A ragged line of scarecrows wearing orange modcotton camp smocks scurried in a moving pocket of darkness. They hadn't changed the algorithmically designed pattern of sweep and stop, each floodlight's gimbals controlled by supposedly faultless software. The clones in the towers had expensive LindyCorp senka goggles for infra and night vision, but afterimages from the burning beams robbed those knockoffs of much utility.

Federal senkas, of much higher quality and several updated designs, would've been better. Coyote spared a toothy smile, plunging into deep cold shadow alongside the Restikkana quonset, where high-value, genetically uncorrupted political undesirables were kept in much larger cages than the shifters. Behind her, very little sound even to her senses–a pebble grinding, a soft exhale, the slight rubbing of cloth against cloth as a wounded appendage was used or braced.

Helga, barely conscious, was now slung between slim dark Korinna and squat, ferociously hairy Joe, whose shift smelled particularly short-tempered as well as bandy-legged. The two of them were idiots, carrying so much baggage... but Coyote, the fingers of her unmutilated hand too small to clasp Natandre's wrist fully yet biting in all the same, was no different.

Their route was circuitous in the extreme, because the small group *also* had to dodge patrols.

Stamping along the main avenues, puffs of dust rising from each polished jackboot's impact, groups of four to six clones bobbed their mask-clad insect heads. Night walks were slightly better than standing guard over euphemistic "work details" during the furnace of late afternoon, but Distarritz was less than half-full now and the so-called quarry probably not worth the effort of poking a shuffling line of chained, ungifted undesirables toward, occasionally popping one in the head with bullet or bolt and afterward enjoying an enhanced liquor ration as well as a half-day's vacation for "preventing an escape."

Words, words, words used to cover up the truth. Yet

people kept talking, even shifters locked in fucking wire cages. It boggled the mind.

Another scramble, bent nearly double and hauling on Natandre. At least the girl kept up, though her beanpole legs were nearly flayed, shinbone flickering white through tears in dirty flesh. Deranian had been working her over pretty good before Coyote provided distraction.

She had to let go of the cargo's wrist because it was time to speed up, bare feet soundless as only a shifter's could be on dry pounded earth and small pebbles. The dark pocket was closing rapidly, and they had to make the end of the next quonset in time—because another lightless space was dilating dead ahead, and it was full of a four-man patrol.

The shift burned in her flesh like sweet alcohol, much finer and smoother than the Mudhole's cheap hooch. Claws out, even her ruined fingers tipped with keratin knives no matter the flagrant use of bio-energy.

Because now was time to survive, and the path lay through the broken bodies of these fash clones, the first one's throat giving in a spray of hot salt crimson and the second going down in a heap from her bare foot ramming into the side of his knee right between ceramo armor plates covered in black fabric.

Any segmented beetle had weak spots. You just had to get a tooth in.

Those two were easy, though, total gimmies. The fourth was the problem because the third had realized something inimical inhabited the pool of shadow in the lee of the equipment shed where they used to drag undesirables for special beatings on Coyote's first Distarritz tour, when the camp was bursting with activity and the reek of death, every quonset packed to the brim.

Even Eppiksally.

The third was raising his stat-rifle and she had to get her claws through his guts, putting him down in time to dissuade the fucking fourth, who could possibly stagger a whole five steps to a grey area where the angle of the building let hot white beamlight sweep by, and the towers couldn't be alerted yet or Coyote, cargo, and every shifter stringing behind them like shit from a pet fish's ass would be pinned down by crossfire.

She had a plan for that eventuality, but it wasn't *ideal*.

Digging, digging, ceramo plate buckling and threatening to screech, she dragged both sets of claws across the midriff, the rifle knocked sideways and somehow anything resembling a trigger finger had been sheared away with a strike she didn't remember making, a burst of volcanic foulness spraying up to her elbows imbued with the massive stink of a clone well-fed on the best ersatz soya and black-market protein his blue ration chits could buy, his abdominal cavity now open to sweet cold night air.

Then she was on the fourth just in time, her shit-slick hands busy with that rifle too, keeping the trigger safe and sound while her bare legs wrapped around the clone's remarkably trim waist, his mask knocked aside as her teeth snapped. She got a mouthful of flesh, dug in, found another, and the crackling as her jaw shifted, jutting forward, was lost in the soft choking sound he made when her snout finally discovered the jugular.

There was another flurry of thumping impacts, snap of breaking bone muffled by ceramo and fabric swathing. The others had clustered clone Number Two, the knee-snapped bastard, who didn't last long.

Coyote half-rose, crouching on the ruin of what had been a tall, strapping blond lord of Distarritz a few heartbeats ago, shaking her shaggy head as she chewed a wad of gristle. Blood steamed, painting cheeks, chin, nose, half her face doused and the front of her orange johnnie soaked with wet copper, mixing with the foulness painting arms and claws.

Breathing behind her, gaunt shifters with their ribs heaving, scent of fear and adrenaline suddenly bearing a high wild sawing edge. Rage, and bloodtaste.

"Everyone okay?" Korinna whispered, barely mouthing two ragged words.

"Shut up," Coyote hissed, quieter than the rising breeze. "Move."

WUNDERBAR

One more patrol–a six-top taken down in near-total silence–
before they reached the spot she wanted. Tacky-wet
clonejuice made the harsh modcotton of Coyote's smock
cling, both crushed and functional hands throbbed–she
didn't have the energy to retract her claws, simply leaving
them out–and her knees were minced from bracing on armor
or pebbled dirt while hauling a clone twice her physical size
back from the bar of white light representing safety or at least
the alerting of his compadres on high. She still felt his fading
struggles in her skinny arms, pressure on the carotid doing its
job and Joe, of all things, darting in to one-two, ribs snapping
under the blows and the clone's cardiac muscle, shocked
beyond tolerances Lindy's mad scientists hadn't designed for,
nearly exploding inside its tough fibrous sac.

Joe was the most competent of the draggers, though
Natandre had flat-stamped one's skull and had to swallow a
yelp as the splintering mask bit her foot, Korinna proved
surprisingly adept at hamstringing, and Abel cooperated with
Sazi in taking out two at once with a deadly silent flurry

ending in dual disembowelments. Even Helga, in a soupy half-daze, crawled to a broken clone aspirating shards of his own piecemeal mask and pressed on his carotid, more an act of silence than mercy.

The stink was hideous, titanic, especially to sharp shifter senses. They all ignored it, clustering in a tight panting knot, Korinna feeling along everyone she could reach, her hot palms checking for anything broken.

Not like she could fix a single shred of damage, but still.

Coyote hunched a slight distance from the puppy pile, dragging in deep rations of wine-sweet desert air. She watched the light beams roving past their last piece of shelter.

Before anyone had truly caught their breath, she shifted on her haunches. "Get ready," she mouthed, and nobody protested. A stiffening ran through the group, shifters becoming individual shapes again. Natandre crept to Coyote's side, somehow managing to seem smaller than her sister.

"You okay?" she whispered.

No. Coyote lifted a shoulder, dropped it. Eyed the expanse of fence and the faltering section of kep behind it–the shimmer fluctuated in a spectrum ungifted couldn't see, since from this direction the wind sent charged particles against the field, causing microsnaps. It would sting like hell and crisp some hair, but they were shifters. Once they were through...

"Almost time." The words were a jailhouse whisper, much softer than the distortion inside a sensa-hood. "When you hit the wire there it'll short out, 'cause the lights are on. Past it, the kep's in flux and it'll sting but less than you think. Go *fast*, go hard, and keep runnin for three klicks and a few more ticks, then turn forty-five degrees southeast and keep going. Before dawn you'll see a big old pile of rock looks like a fuckin antique sailin ship." Her jaw was still half-shifted, slurring the words, so she had to be slow. "Be careful or you'll get shot. Sister's there. Whoever can make it has a chance."

A short silence. Joe snorted–but softly. "You tellin us to run for the wire? That's your plan?"

"What about you?" Korinna wanted to know.

Coyote's head tilted as she listened. The fence patrols were almost equidistant; it was almost, *almost* the moment. Her pulse thumped, heart trying a bit of treacherous lodging in her throat as if the shift had jarred it loose. If they were lucky the snapped wires wouldn't trigger an alarm, nor would the kep feedback knock anyone completely unconscious.

"I'll catch up." Coyote tensed, testing each muscle-string. "Got something personal."

"This isn't personal?" Natandre's long narrow nose twitched. Joe snorted, but again, not very loudly.

"Go." Coyote's hand shot out, digging into Nat's shoulder. She gave a shove toward the moving light beam, the strip of packed barren earth, the fence. "Go. Fast. Now. *Run, you shitheels.*"

They did.

The geography of Distarritz was still carved deep, but in her nightmares it was never this... deserted. Fortunately the howling alarms didn't start when her cargo and the others hit the fences, and the hole torn in the razor wire might even go unnoticed for a patrol pass or two. Once the shifters were out of the shadow Coyote could do nothing more.

She took off in the opposite direction, ducking and dodging, avoiding both roving searchlight beams and clones wandering in packs, each group too concerned with its habitual route to notice anything but the most egregious mistake. It was the dead time of morning, too, when human biorhythms were at their lowest and slowest, when elderly folk slip into the great beyond or the gravely wounded puff out one final, soundless breath.

But for a nocturnal animal the biggest problem was keeping the jitters down, adrenaline and cortisol and other fun hormones flooding her meat, hiking the chances of slip-up or deadrage.

It was the latter she didn't want. Getting shot by clones in Distarritz would be annoying, but she did not fear the long dark. It sounded kind of restful, matter of fact, and she hoped the Lindbergh assertion that shifters, being half animal, didn't have a soul to suffer an afterlife was true.

It would be the only non-falsity to ever spew from that motherfucker's mouth, but even stopped analogs told time once a day, right? She'd never seen a non-digi timepiece, but the saying had to hold a germ of accuracy.

No, what she didn't like the idea of was sliding so far no return was possible, the massive indignity of losing the sole edge she possessed–a reasonable amount of intelligence to match the ruthlessness of whichever half of her held more fury, human or shifter; jury was out on that count.

The deadrage was brutal and effective, but Coyote's pride–insofar as a creature like her could be said to have any–lay in outthinking the entire damn world. Shit and blood and dirt washed off, bones reknit, scars healed, traumas sank with enough booze.

The embarrassment of stupidity was forever.

Most of the camp was a monotony of hunched quonsets, their blank faces regularly drenched with searchlight. There were two rotting warehouses–formerly to hold the belongings of just-delivered undesirables but now probably stuffed with black-market crap meant for enriching clone officers–and the long, blocky "processing" facility, its walls dead black and its roof bearing the shimmer of a personal camo generator plus thermal baffles to fool Federal drones.

The machinery of murder was expensive, after all. Even Deranian's little games weren't nearly so well funded as the assembly line turning undesirables and those just plain unlucky enough to have a high P-factor into pressed blocks of protein and minerals, raw material for more blond Lindbergh bastard-copies.

At least they couldn't make the clones breed yet. Sterile as their murderous maker, which probably drove Lindy out of whatever mind he still possessed.

Distarritz held other anomalies—the water producer, triple-locked as the prison huts rarely were and under double guard 24/7 as well, the guard shelters at the quarry pit, and a few other structures, none of which interested her. No, she headed for the trim Neo-Midcentury cottage in the middle of an artful jumble of boulders impersonating a dry garden.

The old camp commander had once lived a few kliks outside the wire, but regulations had changed a short while before Coyote's first escape. She'd heard about the prisoner labor extracted to construct this abode, the arrangement of the rocks, the processing of the builders en masse before the interior paint had dried.

After all that effort the former commander never even moved in, transferred to a combat unit and his family sent south to a more protected urban area—if there was any large collection of buildings in Lindyland not being drone-bombed lately, that was. As the ranking official, good ol' Dr. D got the cottage while transfer of a new commander was pending, and gossip averred there wouldn't be one, that Deranian had pulled beaucoup strings to get solo housing built *and* rid himself of military oversight.

It would be just like him, Coyote thought, lying

motionless among chunks of stone long drained of daywarmth. No kep field surrounding the house, no patrols stomping past to keep the big man safe and sound. Why bother?

He was the god of this place, and feared nothing.

The cottage had been finished so hastily, the change in command so abrupt, motion sensors or fisheye viz lenses hadn't been installed either and Deranian's arrogance extended to other basic security measures as well. Coyote discovered the pre-escape rumors were true on one point, though–snuggled against the north side of the cottage was a shed-like excrescence, a port just big enough for a well-polished personal transport fueled by petroleo.

Fucking wunderbar. Coyote blinked her good eye several times; the gouged-out socket on the other side ached dully. Her left hand was a mess of meat, only the claws distinct on stubby, truncated fingers. She needed rest, calories, minerals to rebuild bones strip-mined to fuel bursts of furious activity.

One last bit of business.

OWE ME ONE

The front door had a state-of-the-art retinal and print lock, but like a lot of Lindyland, it was simply for show—the windows opened, a luxury the previous commander's family wouldn't have risked their purity by using but had to possess in order to prove their status.

Windows not even wired for alarm the old-fashioned way, in fact. Just locked, and all it took was one claw sawing against glass with the correct pressure to cut out a circle big enough for her right hand. She could do nothing about that small fragile disc hitting the floor, but fortunately the old commandant's spouse had insisted on another cushioning extravagance.

A trail of small, mangled footprints across already fraying etta-poly carpet, a beige probably chosen by said wan, blonde, perpetually pregnant wife. What little furniture remained might have been her choice as well, though Deranian had clearly gotten rid of anything offending his aesthetics—or reminding him of the prior owner. Bare walls with white paint already starting to peel, kitchen with an ancient bamboo dish drainer and prissy pursemouth veneer cabinets plus a breakfast bar and a single wooden barstool only a little nicer than the Mudhole variety, "living" room with a black pleather couch set at a precise distance from the pellet-insert fireplace. The only surprise was the giant oak sideboard huddled against the far wall, as if terrified of both fake flame and petroleo-processed hide.

The urge to dig for a few bottles of cheap alcohol sugars to fuel some healing was faint but definite. Coyote's teeth gleamed, bared to the darkness, and her unwounded eye glittered feverishly.

Carpeted stairs, going down to take advantage of earthen coolness. Creeping with her weight balanced at every moment, alert for creaks or whining wood. Her skin tingled, ears stretching and attempting to twitch in different directions, waiting for the alarms to begin, metallic screaming, jackboots pounding, yells muffled through respirator masks and Distarritz becoming a kicked hive.

There were vast paper-and-mud putawasp complexes in certain parts of the desert, humming to themselves on heatshimmer afternoons. Way back on her first border-crossing she'd led a Lindy patrol toward one, dropping to all fours and already out of danger by the time the clones realized their mistake and the first stingers punctured leather and fabric, finding the spaces between ceramo plates.

And oh, how Coyote had grinned at the screams. Now her expression was thoughtful, remote.

Four smaller, unoccupied bedrooms and a bathroom on the lower level. The thought of taking a shower in precious hot water made a brief, pained twitch cross her thin lips. Her nose wrinkled, a thread of disinfectant and that terrible nauseating cologne thickening as she drifted along, winding through her own simmering shitstink bloodreek.

His scent-image was the same–bleached white collar pressing against papery skin, the narrow colorless eyes and compressed mouth, thin-shaven cheeks and bright scalpel edges. Accompanied by the inaudible grinding of bonesaw and wet rip of tearing flesh, an entire gestalt of Dr. Death, the ruling deity of Distarritz.

Naturally the master bed-and-bath at the end of the hall was his preferred den, but each smaller bedroom was jammed with odd, shrouded shapes–pre-Lindbergh antiques, constructed out of real wood and glass instead of pressed fiber and cloudy, friable gelsheets.

Was he fencing them? Hoarding them? Didn't matter. Coyote stole into the deepest part of the lair, and found out the head demon of Distarritz slept with a nightlight. A whey-faced religious icon in blue and white robes listed from a wall socket, regarding the bedroom with an expression of vacuous horror, her torso glowing gently.

The bed was another pre-Lindy antique, its slick black modsatin sheets clean and soft. Cool air brushed Coyote's torn, naked skin. Carpet scratched her soles luxuriously; her shredded knees softened as she crept, scanning every surface.

A gleaming nightstand, a squat crystalline glass with gently shimmering amber dregs of distilled booze. It smelled enticing.

Her good hand, caked with clotted blood, sandy dirt, and viscera-spill, clamped over Deranian's mouth, pinch-sealing his nose for good measure. Even wasted down to half weight, straps of muscle laid over thinning skeletal girders and her mouth full of the sweetish thick taste of shifter metabolism cannibalizing last reserves, she was stronger.

Little different when I'm not wrapped in filament, huh? She leaned over the bed, batting away his ineffectual, pawing strikes with her mangled left hand. Stupid to sleep on his back, and wallowing on a soft mattress with his head in a vise meant no leverage. He couldn't even kick, trapped in sheets and a light blanket; his fingers were blunt and useless.

Only human, after all.

"Relax," Coyote husked. Felt nearly unnatural to speak normally after all the whispering, to use her real voice in the very heart of Distarritz. "I just need a couple things, Doc, and then I'll be going."

Gurgling cries behind her palm fused to his lips. Her fingers slipped a little, as if she would relent, and his bulging eyes widened further, flaring with hope.

But Coyote had only loosened to tighten at a fractionally better angle, and she beamed mistily at Deranian as the thrashing began to grow desperate, legs and torso swathed in expensive bed linen, arms drown-waving, only slapped aside when they veered too near her face.

She would have liked to linger, to let him think there was a way out. That was one of the worst traps Distarritz laid for prisoners, even the already dead. The idiot body clung to brute survival, the soul folded itself up into smaller and smaller paper animals, mercy and pride shoved into the sewers of what had to be done and eventually atrophying into lace-eaten nothingness.

But it was the mind which tripped you up time and again, scurrying like a rat over stacked bones, serving up one fantastical dream of escape after another. Because it was addicted to hope.

Some Federal propaganda cautioned against becoming Lindylike monsters. Coyote saw nothing wrong with fighting fire with itself. Let the world burn if it was going to be this shitty, let it all go. Nothing mattered. She could easily stay here until they did a camp-wide search, needing their commanding officer for some decision or another, and only let this "genetically pure" sack of organs, meat, and sadism—scanned for chromosome breaks and Novid viral load twice daily, with hypos of largely ineffective "cures" held at the ready—die when they sent the first team of clones down the stairs.

Doc Death's sphincters gave. He fouled the bed, liquid and solid, in a nasty wet gush.

"Fucksake." Coyote sighed, her nose wrinkling almost like Marge's. "You couldn't even wait? Disappointing, Doctor. Very disappointing."

She leaned closer, let one of his fists clip the side of her head. It was like being struck by a sopping-wet washcloth, but gently, no stinging locker-room snap. "So much payback," she crooned, her good eye twitch-blinking, his face chopped into flashes like an old-timey holo in its last stuttering moments before the enclosed power core failed and it was only a palm-size disc to chuck at a small annoyance. "Me, and all the others. You'll have to get most of it in Lindy hell. But before you go..." The dried guck on her face cracked as her expression changed, and even though the petechial starbursts were blooming in his sclera Deranian seemed able to hear her, and redoubled his weakening efforts to get away, to free himself, to breathe.

"Before you go," Coyote repeated, her good eye snapping open, her mouth softening from its rictus-grin, and her thin shoulders relaxing, "I want a few things. For starters, your eye." She leaned a little closer, exquisitely sensitive shifter hearing listening to the laboring thud of his heart, the terrible fading gurgles deep in his throat, the papery sound of *his* eyelids fluttering now.

She could have clamped on his carotid, torn his throat open, disemboweled him through the bedding, but she simply kept her hand where it was, sealed tight as a clone's viral-blocking mask. Softly, thoughtfully, she pursed her lips before saying the last words he would ever hear. "You have to admit you owe me one."

The personal transport was indeed polished to a high gloss, black as a camp guard's boots. A high, wavering mechanical wail began from the towers as she toggled the door latch for the driver's side, careful to keep her claws from punching through metal skin.

Her prison smock left a long smear up the transport's flank, but it was night. Who would notice?

A plush, pleather-coated seat cradled her, conforming to bony hips. She studied the controls for a few moments, taking care to breathe deep and low, attempting to get air all the way to her bellybutton. Hyperventilating now was a mistake, and she couldn't afford even the slightest fuckup.

Her cargo was clear, hopefully following directions with enough lead time on any patrols Distarritz could send out or drones wrested from other tasks. With the commanding officer incommunicado, any order needing his signoff would take several times longer to escape intra-camp channels. They might not even find Deranian for a day or two, being stupid and confused enough to assume he was with his shiny little road-rocket.

It wasn't like a Federal vehicle, but she had the general principles. The only real problem was the fingerlock, easily solved by applying enough pressure with a corpse's hand, still warm, against the biofilm rectangle.

She didn't even need what else she'd cut free–assuming a retinal lock would open to the small gelatinous orb still hot in her ruined left palm, which Coyote didn't think possible.

But waste not, want not. A proverb on both sides of the border.

Searchlights swiveled frantically atop the towers, stabbing the innocent, uncaring night. The guard barracks were emptying, swarms of hastily masked clones spilling out like putawasps or frightened ants, the kep field suddenly coruscating sheets past the wire, its stubby pillars flushing deep, angry red. The weak spot near the dead bit of wire–and that was luck, too, she'd gambled that camp maintenance had ignored that particular task since she hadn't used that exit on her first escape attempt, being somewhat more hurried– would only be a few shades paler than its siblings on either side.

The engine caught, triggered by a lever instead of a button. She couldn't smell the burst of burning carbon because the transport's interior was sealed; it was presumed both driver and any passengers would be wearing nose filters and mouthshield for the short trip from the house's side airlock to the open shed-port. A wonderland of colorful symbols and buttons glowed on the dash, but Coyote simply tossed the eye and mannequin-limp amputated hand into a center console dish–perfectly placed for holding a drink or snack while tooling along on roads cleared after each drone strike by chain-ganged undesirables–and curled her own fingers around the right side of the steering yoke. There was the accelerator pedal, and the wider one was the brake. The shift lever echoed Federal design, and she bit her lip while figuring out the park-locking mechanism.

Fucksticks, Lindys gotta make everything so fuckin difficult, get with the fuckin times. She kept bellybutton-breathing.

Now it was time for the real trick. Everything else in the plan hinged on this.

The park-lock released, the engine roared. Coyote

pressed the accelerator; the transport, startled, leapt forward. It veered between garden-boulders, bumped up onto the packed dirt of a camp "street," and she pointed it for the main thoroughfare.

She didn't even realize she was muttering.

"Just passin through, just passin through, just passin through..."

PASSIN THROUGH

Front lights blazing with halogen fury, Doctor Deranian's private vehicle slewed wildly through scattering groups of guards, officers, maintenance staff, plus a few disoriented or screaming medical techs who thought the Federal Army had arrived and their next stop was a publicly broadcast tribunal for fash warcrimes–if they weren't shot on sight.

A strapping officer, his shoulder pips winking when hit by craze-looping searchlight beams but his martial demeanor somewhat impeded by the fact that he had scrambled outside both raving drunk and without his trousers, skidded to a stop in front of the transport and held his arms wide. Perhaps he was even screaming at the camp's priority commchannel inside his hastily affixed mask, but Coyote hadn't touched the button with the wifi-comm symbol on it.

The accelerator was mashed to the floor, both good hand and nearly pulped one fused to the steering yoke, and she now had a feel for how this stupid-ass cart behaved in motion with its funny air-filled rubber rounds instead of proper antifrik cells. The ride was smoother than perching on

Chicken, but she preferred the DONQ unit's habit of attempting to buck her loose whenever its algorithms suspected her attention had wandered.

Not that she rode him very often. That space was for cargo, whether it was a bounty, a load of contraband, or some sad sack who happened to catch a skinny-ass shifter on a good—or bad—day.

Her arms trembled, but the transport didn't care. It locked onto the pantsless officer like a thermal drop from a fully loaded drone and roared as it plowed right into him, tossing the clone's body an astonishing distance skyward.

"PASSIN THROUGH!" Coyote yelled, her good eye nearly incandescent and the socket on the other side throbbing wetly as specialized tissues sought to close, heal, regrow. "GET OUTTA THE FUCKIN WAY!"

Quonsets flashed by on either side. Could those caged inside hear the ruckus? What would the gossip say? The whispers just below mic threshold as shifters swallowed the agony of trapped stillness, the soft words passed along a shuffling line of ungifted, single-skinned undesirables as they trudged to the next labor detail, the mutters in holding cells or rocking, swaying lo-frik railcars?

Maybe nobody except Coyote would ever know about this, like the night sky just after her first escape as she crawled along the floor of a gully, claws digging furrows through sandy soil and the mangled stumps of her feet throbbing with wet agony, dry particles working into lacerated flesh. She'd had to saw and grind instead of cleanly slicing because they'd left her shackled on a Nekksandra table overnight after she'd been caught working at the faulty lock on her cage door.

Rolling onto her back, seeing those dry diamond fires scattered across the world's dark roof, listening for the alarms to start in the distance or the thumping mechanical sound of sniffer 'bots…

The front gate was lit up like the big winter festival tree in every Fed-Mexi town's Plaza de la Libertad. The towers weren't shooting yet, though a few searchlights had locked on to Deranian's vehicle. The clones couldn't decide whether to shit or go blind; if they ventilated a commanding officer the chances of ending up in a frontline penal battalion were better than even, and—

"COME ON!" Coyote screeched. "COME ON, HIT ME, I WANT YOU TO HIT ME!"

The transport's engine howled in response. More tumbling fleshy impacts on the hood or against the side, a jolt as air-filled rubber rounds passed over an unfortunate body tripped and sprawling on the main thoroughfare, beads and post-mounted speakers blatting with high-decibel dismay—nobody in Distarritz was sleeping tonight.

Nobody except Deranian.

"TRICK OF THE YEAR!" Coyote, near-delirious with glee, didn't know she was screaming. "WATCH THIS, LINDBERGH! I'M FUCKIN PASSIN THROUGH!"

The vehicle barreled through the reinforced front gate of Distarritz at nearly 130 kph. The two horizontal bars meant to deter such traffic snapped and went flying, the guards on either side stared or swore, paralyzed, and as crimson rear lights glowed through a trail of dust someone in a tower finally had the presence of mind to open fire on what they could only assume was Doctor Death, heading to hell at last.

It was far too late.

Paving rose and dipped with a not-unpleasant hum under the rubber rounds, a soporific song. Coyote's vision swam, a hot fingertip tracing down her crusted cheek. She eased off the accelerator, staring at the speed display and wondering blankly why it was in ancient, stupid imperial instead of easy metric.

Fucking fash hated anything reasonable.

The vehicle's engine was making a strange noise though its fuel gauge was at half-cell, which was probably enough but she didn't know the drain on petroleo... Was it *tanks*? It was a liquid, it had to be in a tank.

What the fuck are you doing?

Right. Conversions. Speed, approximate time, distance. Was she far enough away yet?

The vehicle's interior smelled like Deranian. Faintly, to human noses, but the stink was deep and prickling to a shifter, contaminated with blood and fearsweat.

Her foot lifted from the accelerator. Gravity and friction began their work in earnest. The transport rocked, its engine-thrum settling into a different rhythm with a more pronounced, somewhat irregular knocking. Coyote glanced down at the center console, instrument glow from the dash more than adequate to show the wet gleam of a slowly collapsing eyeball. It had rolled around to peer at her, iris and pupil clouding rapidly, long nerve-string trailing behind. The hand claw-chopped from Deranian's right arm was stiffening, too.

For a bare moment she considered popping the eye in her mouth and chewing, a wet salt burst with a touch of copper from hemorrhage, no different than any gift of fresh carrion to a starving desert creature. Meat was meat, she was possibly too exhausted to hunt, and she needed calories. Any would do.

Yet in the end she watched the speed drop, drop further, and reached for the door's emergency latch before her brain was ready. The conversions were still running but the tired animal of her body knew better, gauging by the pressure of velocity and the rasping against her dirt-crusted nape. She pulled both legs up, thought about getting a foot on the console, played out the movement a few times in the soup her brain was rapidly becoming.

A savage yank, her claws shearing plasteel, metal, sealant, and insulation, and she pushed herself sideways. Even a weakened, famished shifter was much stronger than a plain old ungifted, and she managed to *not* hit the steering yoke with knees or toes as she was flung from the vehicle, which continued merrily along the road, weaving slightly. It could bump over the shoulder and veer into desert, fine. Its standard-issue tracking beacon would do the rest.

She landed badly, the hard crust of dried effluvia and dirt not helping at all, the rags of her camp smock even less. The only way to take the blow was ragdoll-limp, shifter flexibility and instinct using adjustments too tiny to be conscious. A plume of dust in the transport's wake, its rear lights glowering bloody through the haze; smaller puffs rising in her own.

A second-to-last piece of luck was neither fencing, nor boulders, nor cacti near the road, more good fortune than Coyote would have thought possible if there was room in her battered body for anything other than pain and a stinging wash of bleak stunned irritation at the fact of continued existence. Her heart still worked, lungs still heaved, a couple bones gave sharp twinges meaning incipient or hairline fracture, and physics finally decided to stop fucking with her, leaving an insect sprawled at the bottom of a cup staring at tiny holes in night's inverted sieve. A great light lurked behind those shimmering pinpricks, pressing against the darkness like a cat eager to strop its chosen owner's leg.

In the east, a faint suggestion of pale grey had begun.

Dawn was a ways off, true, but was comin round the mountain. Coyote lay, staring at the holes in the colander slapped over this part of the world, and the faint tremors in her chest between great gasping breaths was not pain, not fear.

It hurt too much to laugh, but the quivers would not stop. The plan had worked.

She had escaped Distarritz for the second time.

INCIDENTAL, MIRACLE

Half in shift, a wounded creature scuttled across boulder-strewn sand, dodging spiny plants, its shadow melding with theirs only to separate a moment later. It moved with lurch-lolloping almost-grace from one form of cover to the next, pausing briefly when something small and too slow for its own good skittered across its path.

A couple furry orange-and-black spiders with fungal growths on their backs, a scorpion whose tail jabbed deep into the web between thumb and forefinger causing a pleasant tingle as venom was neutralized, a rattler too sluggish with cold and successful night hunts to slither away from another night-silent hunter–even a patch of mineral-rich dirt in the lee of a particular stone was plundered, two fistfuls crammed in Coyote's mouth because her nose said whatever the black powder-crumble was loaded with would help with bones becoming too brittle for the demands of enhanced musculature.

Crunching on the rattler al fresco helped too. Even the

keratin of the rattle-scales could be used by her greedy, needy body.

For all that, she couldn't take more than incidental prey. The eastern horizon bore a white line now, sand and hardpan turning grey and blue, shadows becoming more definite. For a short while yips and howls echoed in the middle distance, and she weighed the prospect of veering aside, seeking shelter with cousins.

But they had their own problems, and once she was curled up in a den, she might decide to never leave. Which wouldn't be so bad. What kept her plodding onward toward a pile of rock no different than the other irregular outcroppings?

From this direction, it didn't look like an antique sailing ship but a flattened torso with two spines jutting through. The sky was still crystal-clear—whatever drones had been put to the task of finding Deranian's transport were probably proceeding in the general direction the vehicle had been pointed, due south toward faraway Federal lines as if a punch-drunk escapee was rabbiting.

Mouth dry as Distarritz's punishment pit, she couldn't even salivate at the longing thought of a bunny too slow to escape a wounded predator. Which was funny as fuck, really.

Maybe the world was embarrassed to look on all this bullshit, because the sky began to flush.

Anyone who thinks a desert is lifeless don't know shit, and should be dropped into one at dawn. Night-patrol stragglers coming home, the day crew gearing up for work before noonglare makes movement a matter of slithering into whatever shade can be found, pops and crackles as the temperature begins to rise, air fleeing the horizon-blister swelling to birth the sun's pitiless eye—as symphonies went it wasn't bad, but she preferred a few corridas and a cold beer, her boots propped on a junked car while she contemplated a long day's sleep in a safe bolthole.

Suddenly a sharp slope reared before her. Coyote's head jerked up, scanning in either direction, thin shoulders hunching. Her fur was patchy, the slashes on her knees showing white cartilage, one hand a stump with claws, no fluid available to let the hematomas all over her begin to swell and push out the damage, preparing for healing.

She turned and worked along the base of the rise, looking for a particular configuration of cactus near a wind-whittled rock like a grinning, hunchbacked old woman, her shawl knotted at the right shoulder. An abuela who didn't bother hiding, simply sat and waited for those who looked closely enough.

Just like death.

Fuck. Coyote didn't have the energy to say it aloud. She faced the slope once more—nearly vertical, loose scree, stunted vegetation cowering wherever a scrap of dew or infrequent precipitation could be caught or eked out. Hidden in one of the folds was a hole choked by two tough, spiny olive-leaved shrubs.

The back door. Now all she had to do was climb.

Margery crouched easily at the mouth of the cave, watching mornlight strengthen to flood the desert. It had a certain sere beauty, sure, but she still preferred beaches or rolling, more temperate hills. The only green here was dusty and greyish, and though she liked subtle, restful variations in taupe and beige, the heat and the sand creeping into every crease were powerful inducements to move elsewhere.

The DONQ unit carried quite a few medical supplies and a huge load of vitamin-enriched protein bars, as if the runner had guessed the needs of half a dozen or so famished, brutalized shifters. The feline who seemed to be in charge divvied up small portions at regular time intervals, and insisted the fellow who had taken the duty of chief complainer–a canid, but one who seemed nearly reasonable under his carapace of bluster–also take care of corralling the spent packaging, folding it neatly and filling a couple of Hickam bags, that necessity for in-country disposal.

Coyote had apparently thought of everything. Except her own escape.

"I cannot believe you left her there," Margery repeated. But softly, as if talking to herself.

"Would *you* have argued with her?" Natandre shuddered, plastered to her sister's side despite the disparity in height and body mass. The high-grade protein was doing her good; bruises were going down, but every Distarritz shifter was a bag of bones. It would take more than a few bars to replace lost muscle.

And more than simple escape to fix whatever psychological wounds lingered, but that was a problem for down the line. Frankly, Marge hadn't expected to get this far, even with the stubbornness her shift was known for.

Of all the bad things–the breaching of their hiding spot, the beatings in an Old Houston basement, the goddamn Lindy bureaucrat with his "deal," the torment of the idea that she was either leaving her sister to die above the border or would have to betray an innocent person to get Natandre back, the trip south into Federal territory, the search for a runner who would take the job, the sheer insanity of Coyote's plan–the worst had been waiting for days in this goddamn cave, patting the walls and memorizing the stone over and over while the DONQ unit's surveillance blur hummed to itself.

Don't fuckin move, Coyote had snarled. *Do not fuckin rabbit. You follow the fuckin route and you* stay *there with fuckin Chicken. You move when that light on his panel goes red* or *when I come and tell you to fuckin pack up, you got it? Repeat it, bitch.*

And then hearing stealthy scrabble on the slope below, whispers passed back and forth–she'd reached for the rifle, certain it was a Bloc patrol, and nearly opened fire before realizing one of the voices was familiar.

It was a certified miracle in a deeply unmiraculous world. *Bugfuck*, everyone said about Coyote, and certainly the woman's personality had little to recommend it. Yet Natandre was alive and breathing, snuggled against her sister. There were other shifters, who swore the runner had been with them in Distarritz and had gotten them out.

The light on the panel, visible on the DONQ unit's side because its cover had been pulled aside, had not turned red yet.

"We should get the fuck gone," the canid complainer muttered.

"Not during daylight." Korinna, the feline in charge, had the patience of a saint or a primary-school teacher. "How's Helga doing?"

"Helga is fucking miserable," the most badly wounded shifter–also canid, Margery thought, though it was difficult to tell when she stank of blood and injury–croaked. "But alive, thank you."

"You think she got out?" Abel, the lone ophidia shifter, lay supine near the cave wall, probably drawing strength from contact with mothering earth. "Man, bitch is *crazy.*"

"Bugfuck," Margery corrected. "I didn't believe she'd..."

"How much did you pay her?" Natandre wriggled slightly,

pressed her cheek against Marge's shoulder. "Where did you get enough? What did you do?"

Two hundred doesn't cover this. It doesn't even come close. "I fixed the DONQ unit," she was forced to say, lamely. "And... they said things, about her. That she takes jobs nobody else will."

"Just passin through," the canid said, and gave a soft, chuffing laugh. They spoke in peculiar whispers, as if afraid of being heard even there. "Why'd she go back, for fucksake?"

"When *do* we move?" Korinna was focused on more practical affairs. They were still in the Bloc, after all. There were kilometers of open desert and the front line to surmount, and...

"When the light turns red," Marge said. "Or when she gets back."

"Prolly dead," the complainer muttered, and turned back to his folding of wrappers when everyone stared at him. Even Helga moved her head and blinked in his direction, and the sudden thick silence was full of survivors' shame.

Marge was about to speak, but the DONQ unit, placid and unmoving once they reached this particular cave halfway up the rock face, suddenly quivered. It turned to face the rear of the stone hollow, metal hooves delicately avoiding both unpacked supplies and Korinna's crouching form. A horizontal crack in the back wall was full of sour inky blackness, exhaling a dry breath at random intervals as the wind shifted. Margery could sense the lightless chambers beyond, and might have liked to go exploring under different circumstances–especially if the crack could be widened, since she'd have to shift to get her hips through.

"Whafuck," the ophidia shifter breathed, and rolled painfully onto his side, shutting up when the complainer shot him a filthy glance.

Outside, dawn was well underway, the desert singing its morning aria. Slight scrabbling noises came from the horizontal crack; the DONQ unit's ears were up and perked far forward, scanning. None of its lights turned red, though. In fact, a few turned green, and a single LED at the bottom left of the panel flashed white, intermittently at first before settling into regularly spaced heartbeats.

Korinna reached for a rifle jutting up from one of the unopened packs. The DONQ unit's left ear flicked, and it twitched slightly, a restless, warning movement.

"*Fuuuuuuuck.*" An eerie half-moan, half-whisper slid from the crack. "Fuuuuuuuck... meeeee... shiiiiit..."

Margery shook free of Natandre's arm around her waist and padded through the cave. She peered into the darkness, her nose twitching.

"Is it a ghost?" Nat whispered.

"No ghost," Margery said, and her pulse throbbed in chest, wrists, and even her ankles, safely encased in military-surplus boots Coyote had picked up from the filthy fucker in his shiny silver trailer.

Miracle.

A thin stream of sand, a falling pebble dropped from the crack's lower lip. The orifice drooled a bit more gritty dust, another slightly larger piece of stone, then a skinny, battered shape in an orange Lindyland prisoner johnnie like all the others'–though significantly filthier, and reeking of carnage–wriggled through.

Coyote would have hit the floor, but Margery darted close, batting aside a reflexive punch from a scarecrow-skinny fist, and caught her. The runner looked worse than Helga, a collection of bones and teeth, one feverish dark eye protruding from a crusted face, and her expression was a skull's cheerful grimace, sardonically amused by the answer to life's great riddle.

"Saints," Margery breathed, cradling the wasted form. Burning with fever, barely held together, the runner blinked slowly once, twice.

"Fuck no," Coyote croaked. Her ribs heaved, stick-legs dangling. "You fucks... better not... have eaten... all the Jvstin... bars."

MY PROBLEM NOW

Chicken greeted her the usual way, head snaking out and teeth snapping; Coyote's punch between his eyes wasn't up to her usual standard but still rattled his robotic brains a good bit. "Fucker," she murmured, nearly affectionately. "Missed you too." She cast an eye over the baggage–good, they hadn't descended on it like a hungry crowd on ration-delivery day.

The supply of potable water was too precious to waste on washing, but her clothes and her fringed jacket were reasonably fresh. Once she scraped the worst of the dry crust from her skin–an operation performed while jamming whole protein bars in her mouth and chewing methodically–she could get dressed.

Marge hovered uncertainly, just as large but not quite in charge at the moment. In fact, she wore a look Coyote had seen on many a cargo's face–relief and grudging admiration, which was fine, except for what inevitably followed.

Cargo ended up fearing and despising runners, not least because so many who crisscrossed the border didn't give a rat's ass about anything but profit. It was also safer for scared cargo to lash out at the closest target, a psychological reflex shifters and the ungifted shared in spades. On a run they worshipped you. In town, they'd sell you to Federal or fash quicker than liquid shit running downhill.

Her teeth soaked up minerals, her bones still aching but not quite so deeply. Coyote bit off the tab on a packet of rehydration gel and sucked at it while buttoning the long-sleeved modflannel shirt over the thermal waffleweave under. It was nice to be clothed again, even if the dirt rubbed into her hide itched relentlessly.

The rest of the group except for Marge would have to make the run in raggedy-ass orange Distarritz prison smocks, but there was an alkaline pool nearby to dip those in for bleaching and at least they had something to chew on. She hadn't really expected to bring out more than one or two shifters–Natandre had been the job, anyone else ballast she didn't need.

But fuck it all, whatever. Coyote sucked on the gel packet, calculated the remaining food and hydration, gazed at the medical supplies with her good eye. The empty socket itched furiously, but repairs would be slow. Her body had other priorities.

Once she was laced into her own familiar boots–Marge had turned her in wearing a second-best outfit and a cheap pair of surplus hooves, since Coyote knew anything she arrived wearing was as good as incinerated–the short-term energy flush from reaching a goal and swallowing a calorie load was fading fast. So she tapped a few buttons on Chicken's panel, closed the hatch cover, and yawned, hugely. At least now the air whistling past didn't make her fuckin broken teeth hurt, which was a blessing.

"We move just after sunset," she announced. "You're my fuckin cargo now, I'll get you over the border. Once that's done you go to a man named Fassby—Marge over there knows him—and you tell 'im the ugly bitch sent you. He'll slide you into Federal reentry the right way, no fake papers, there's relief programs for medical attention and short-term stipend, too. But before then, you're my fuckin problem, so you do what I say when I say it. If you fuck up or make any play to alert a drone or patrol, I'll fuckin kill you myself. Other than that, just keep your head down and follow orders." Her throat burned, too much talking. "Get some rest."

The fringes on her jacket whispered a welcome as she wrapped it hard around her wasted frame and settled at the very back of the cavern, under the crack she'd crawled through forty-five minutes ago. She closed her eyes, forced a few bellybutton-deep breaths, and fell into a thin grey restorative doze.

It wouldn't do to sleep *too* soundly.

Soft movement as the others arranged themselves. Then Korinna whispered, just under mic threshold.

"So, uh... does she have a name, or are we not supposed to know?"

"Ask her when she wakes up," Marge replied in a hot, sibilant undertone. "I dare you."

FULL OF SURPRISES

At least they'd used enough of the supplies that Chicken could carry Helga, who turned out to be a dark-haired dog-flavor shifter with a perpetually uncertain smile plastered to her even-featured face. Joe was also canid—he'd get along just great with Weimmar and his crew—Korinna was feline, and Abel a relatively rare slitherfolk. Sazi and Beulah rounded out the group, narrow-nosed and beady-eyed, nervous like rodentia shifters always were.

They only relaxed around their own kin.

For all that, shifters were easier than the ungifted. At least they had the sense to do what she told them, knew to keep their hands to themselves, and none of them crowded her—except for Marge, who seemed to think she was at least partly in charge of the whole operation instead of just Natandre and her own ample-bosomed self.

They moved with reasonable quiet through nights full of dusty, braid-tangled gullies and ravines, Chicken's blur bouncing off rock on either side to foil any passing drone's infra- and night-scans. They also stayed where Coyote put them when she veered away to hunt, coming back with small game to be eaten raw and whole.

None of the Distarritz shifters caviled at that, even Nat. Marge looked a little green, but she didn't need the calories at the moment so it was a moot point.

Coyote's teeth crunched bones, savoring each bit of remineralization. Hot preyblood helped with salt and thirst, muscle and organs filling her body's different cravings and needs. Still, she could only hunt a little, and their supply of protein bars was dwindling fast.

Four days spent holed up in caves, emerging near dusk to spend long nights hiking uncomplaining through the chill. Five, six. Rumble of artillery in the distance, where it shouldn't be unless the rumors of another offensive were true.

That was worrisome, and Coyote chewed over the problem while walking, slept as it revolved inside her skull, barely tasted her portions of two jackrabbits and a scrawny, unwary bird while crouching next to Chicken on the ninth day. The bandage over the wet hollow of her slowly regrowing eye was an irritant, but better than sand in the socket.

It was about the time for cargo to start getting nervous ideas, and the surprise was Korinna—instead of Joe—edging closer while Coyote sucked the marrow from a thigh bone, luxuriating in the taste.

"We're moving east." Korinna hunched nervously just out of range, as if wary of earning a claw-swipe or hissed warning to stay away from another shifter's food.

Marge, crouched next to her sister, was watching. Perhaps uneasily, since her forehead was furrowed under messy, dust-stiff dark hair, the now dye-free stripe near-glowing in scant moonlight. The rest of the Distarritz shifters hunched over their portions just as Coyote did.

Eating was serious business. Korinna must have wolfed her ration without bothering to chew.

Coyote nodded, a single drop-and-rise of her pointed chin. Clothes were also a luxury; the others had to be feeling vulnerable right now. Every minute spent in Lindyland was a risk, even in uninhabited areas. Drones and patrols didn't have to be everywhere; they just had to catch enough folk to keep rumors going and the fear fresh enough to force stupid mistakes.

"East," Korinna repeated. "Not south."

Coyote let the marrow slide easily down her throat. "You hear that?" She pitched the words loud enough to be heard by all her cargo. "That's artillery, and the pattern means another offensive. You wanna run through that, go ahead. Might even make it, if neither side gets hold of you in the active zone. I can feed the rest of them easier without whiners eating good rations."

The feline shifter's cheekbones stood out starkly; she'd be a looker at full weight once the scars from Deranian's attentions paled. Long and lithe, burning with shifter vitality, and if her hair regrew a bit there would be no shortage of amorous attention directed her way. "I didn't mean it like that."

"You sure?" Coyote showed her teeth, decorated with strands of bunny fur. The keratin digested just like everything else. "Already didn't plan on bringing more than Nat out. Rest of you are ballast."

Korinna lifted both hands, crescents of sand-grime under her nails and in her palm-creases. Must just drive her batty; felines liked being clean. "I'm sorry. I was curious."

Sure you were. "Go be curious somewhere else," Coyote said, but the snarl was only half-hearted. She didn't miss Marge's tension, the way she had eased Nat aside and gathered herself, relaxing by degrees only when Korinna rejoined Joe a few meters away, the canid slurping at his own food, his eyes gleaming while he watched the entire situation play out.

It could be Marge was worried their runner was going to take offense and leave the entire group stranded; some even made a profit that way. There was even a small chance she was ready to back Coyote up like before, which was awful nice of her.

Yes, ol' Margie was full of surprises. Coyote's grin changed a few fractions, her tongue busy working at fur caught in her teeth, and she held the other woman's dark, thoughtful gaze.

Near dawn two days later, just as dew began to settle over cactus, rock, and sand alike, Coyote's head jerked up. She scanned the sky–what could be seen, at least, since a ravine's walls drew close on either side, its floor wide as two camp processing chutes.

Chicken halted too, head held high, and the tip of his right ear began to swivel. The tiny vibration of the gimbal responsible for the movement was all the warning she needed even if her own senses hadn't caught the sudden unsound, fine hairs prickling all over her.

"What is it?" Margie whispered from her post at Chicken's hindquarters, casting worried glances at her sister on the other side and making sure Helga didn't tip from the perch.

The Distarritz shifters, in loose file behind them, crowded close. Korinna and Joe took rearguard, which suited Coyote fine.

"Shhh." But then she figured they probably deserved a word of caution. "Drones. Stay close, in Chicken's blur."

They continued, the DONQ unit's ear-tip adding a faint sibilance to the desert's expectancy. The hairs didn't go down, though, and Coyote grew more uneasy, glancing upward every so often, rubbing her still-bruised hands together—bones and deeper wounds received the bulk of calorie-fueled healing, her left paw was still misshapen—and occasionally kissing what remained of the first knuckle on that side, hoping for luck.

They'd had all the good fortune this run was gonna give, though. She heard the first explosions just as Chicken let out a warning snort, stealth laid aside in favor of security.

For some reason, motherfuckers—of one side or the other—were on a bombing run over this deserted slice of sand. Maybe Chicken's blur was pinged with some new tech, maybe there were enemy troops in the area, maybe some Chair Force joystick jockey made commander had simply triangulated the wrong patch of battlefront, maybe the offensive was starting a push through this forsaken piece of wilderness.

There was precedent, after all. Not that it mattered.

"RUN!" Coyote bellowed, and bolted for the end of the ravine.

CLEAR, CRYSTAL

The end of the narrow defile was a wall of packed boulders, but Coyote turned hard left and plunged through a timber-framed aperture a little over two meters high and almost as wide, a piece of night left stuck in a hillside as the eastern horizon gave birth to another day. The wood was old, probably seasoned enough to go up like a torch if a match or sigga-light was held to it, and every few meters down the black throat was another doorframe of same design.

But there was no way of seeing that. The passageway was utterly dark, even to shifter eyes; moving air told Coyote there wasn't an obstruction for some while and in any case, it was cover. If the rest of the tunnels held up...

Chicken was hard on her heels, his leash algorithm unhampered by pressure sensors telling him living cargo was on his back; his legs blurred as they shortened enough to avoid scraping Helga on the roof. Marge and Nat couldn't fit in the passageway at the same time and were forced to drop back, a temporary clot at the door resolved at high speed as rolling thunder swept over the ravine behind them.

The earth shook, thin rivulets of dirt cascading down to patter like rain. Grit stung Coyote's eye, fingered her hair, hit the back of her throat as she inhaled. Sazi and Beulah were screaming, Joe cussing with astonishing fluidity and facility that almost cheered Coyote up, Abel grimly silent, and Natandre sobbed as Helga repeated *oh shit oh shit ohshitshitshit* like a catechism.

"LIGHTS!" Coyote screamed, forging ahead. "CHICKEN, FUCKIN LIGHTS!"

The DONQ unit obliged; a reddish glow dilated from its sides, brighter crimson beams from its oculars, swiveling as it scanned. The tunnel shook and thin threads of sand kept falling, but military ingenuity held up great when desert desiccation was at hand to preserve its work.

The tunnel widened just as the rumble-shaking abated. Coyote skidded to a stop, which meant Chicken did too, Helga windmilling atop his stub-shortened frame to keep her balance. Marge's hand shot out and she grabbed Natandre, who looked fit to zoom right past Coyote and into the darkness. Sazi nearly plowed into the DONQ's hind end.

Korinna was last to appear, pressing a hand against her left side, her eyes huge and near-senseless, mouth working silently. She nearly ran into Joe; Abel and Beulah threw themselves on the feline to slow her down. A short flurry of movement later they all huddled around Chicken, red light turning skin liverish and lips purple, bleached orange smocks now a fetching puce and flapping stiffly.

Coyote counted them down, halted next to the feline. "Shrapnel? How bad?"

"No." Korinna's teeth gleamed as she bared them, peeling her hand away from the side of her abdomen. "Just... muscle pain. Stitch."

"Your electrolytes are fucked up." Coyote dug in Chicken's

packs, pressed a packet of rehydration gel into the feline's feverish palm. "Take that. Joe, make sure she does. Rest of you, everyone find a buddy and hold hands, just like in primary. Margie, your buddy's Helga, keep 'er on Chicken. We gotta move."

"About half of this is bored through caliche." Margie sounded tentative, as if she expected Coyote to take offense. "Immigration?"

"Some of it's natural–an aquifer sinking, I heard. The rest was sappers." At least they could talk now. There was more saturation bombing going on, but thankfully not directly overhead. The constant low grinding mixed with a whisper of artillery at more distance, nothing close enough to be concerning, not yet. "From all the way back, uh, fourth year of the war, I think? Widening and venting, whole thing was for moving supplies when they were gonna do a fancy sickle maneuver or some shit. Didn't work out. Runners been using 'em since–and patrols, so if we meet someone you shut the fuck up and let me handle it."

"Handle it," Marge repeated, thoughtfully. "You, uh, want your rifle? And should I carry the other one?"

At least she was trying to help. "Blast down here might cause a cave-in." Coyote halted, peering into the dimness. "It's sharps in the dark or leaving each other the fuck alone, so most of the time everyone chooses option B."

Which was ultimately true... but also simplistic. During an offensive, things below could get just as dodgy as above. If they started walking the big guns directly overhead to clear the way for a mecha-armored thrust, a good old cascading collapse could set in as well. Year Four was a long time ago, even if neither side seemed able to overcome the other. Some parts of the tunnels might indeed be migration work from before secession, back when Lindbergh was just a crazy rich coot funding "research" and buying his way into politics, El Norte a myth of milk and honey.

Huh. Strange, how her memories of "before the war" were so fuzzy and indistinct. No use in remembering the inessential, not with so much else to keep track of.

Still, she hadn't expected Distarritz to be so... empty. Maybe Looney Lindy and his happy helpers were running out of resources; they'd killed at least as many of their own as they had Federals or Cascadia-Transcanada Allied.

None of which made a shit-bite worth of difference at the moment. The tunnel bifurcated here. Left or right? Chicken had incomplete maps, worse than useless in this quadrant. He also had scanning capability, but if anyone overhead got pings from underground, they might bring in thermal pounders and turn Coyote and her cargo to paste, along with anyone else unfortunate to be down here at the moment.

"Ky?" Marge, a little closer now.

Coyote blinked and spun, her ruined hand throbbing as claws lengthened. The paw was re-forming, still a snarled mess of bone fragments attempting to align, tendons trying to find their homes, muscles seeking repair, blood supply sluggish and infection only barely staved off. She restrained the urge to strike, but only barely. "Whafuck?"

"Which way you wanna go?" The stripe in Marge's hair shone through the dirt, and her nice wide shoulders were very loose, considering. Even with half her face in shadow and the other dipped in red emergency light–Chicken wouldn't run out of solar charge for a long while yet–she looked remarkably relaxed.

"Chicken's got maps of other sections." Coyote normally wouldn't discuss this shit with cargo; a runner was the authority until the job was finished, no discussion sought or tolerated. But she was a fraction more rattled than she wanted to admit, even to her own bitchy little self. "Been through here before, there's four or five safe routes. But..."

"But." Margie nodded, thoughtfully. "Hold on."

She glided forward, examined both passageways. Ran her hands along the timber framing, tested the walls—acid-bored stone in some parts, rock-packed dirt refusing collapse out of sheer stubbornness in others—with her fingertips.

"It's okay," Natandre whispered to her fellow escapees, a similar stripe glinting in her own close-cropped hair. "This is way better than *up there*."

"Says you." Joe didn't sound happy.

"Thought dogs liked dens." Abel's laugh was thin and pale, but cheerful enough. Beulah laughed, and Sazi snorted a half-giggle.

Marge returned; no more twitching, and the nervous blinking was gone. "Where you wanna go?" she repeated. "I mean, which direction are we aiming?"

"South two klicks, slight jag east at the end of about half a klick. Could be more if there's cave-in damage. And things down here aren't like above. They *move*." She glared with her good eye, daring the other woman to scoff. "The tunnels change around. Find shit you wouldn't believe tucked in corners—old-timey, even, from way before petroleo."

She expected Joe to say something like *fuckin kid stories,* but maybe the bombing and the red light, not to mention fatigue and hunger, were keeping him from being more than moderately annoying. Or maybe it was the way Margie nodded immediately.

"I believe it," she said quietly. "Stone remembers things. Two klicks south and half east, huh? Then we want that tunnel." She pointed at the left doorway. "The other one's probably a shorter route but I don't like how it feels. Cave-ins, probably. Just not good."

Well, sonofabitch. Coyote studied Marge's half-hidden face. No trace of arrogance or falsity, but then again, her precious sister would die with everyone else if things went to shit down here.

"Fine. You take point, but if you smell anything other than dirt or if I say, you drop the fuck back in a hurry. Clear?"

"Crystal." Marge didn't snap a salute, but it looked like she was tempted for a bare second.

"Stay close to Chicken," Coyote told the rest. "Try not to breathe too hard."

Nobody laughed. Which was probably just as well.

PART FOUR
THE FINISH

FINISH THE RUN

Slowly but steadily, pausing only to sniff deeply, Marge the large and in charge slipped through the tangle of passageways. Once she had them scramble over half a fall-in, Chicken shifting to hover instead of legs and having to be hauled over the hill of debris. Helga said she could walk, but Coyote ordered her back up on the DONQ unit.

"Save it for later," she said, nearly wheezing from the amount of dust in the air. The temperature was ticking up, whether from shifters with high metabolisms shedding heat in a confined space or for some other reason. Occasionally a cooler draft tiptoed past, usually at junctions where Margie chose a direction without breaking stride, sometimes trailing her fingertips over the wall on one side or another.

Joe was occupied with keeping Korinna from hyperventilating; Abel herded Sazi and Beulah with languid gestures. Next to Marge and Natandre, he was most comfortable with their current environment; the two rodentia didn't quite mind close quarters but jumped nervously whenever the barrage or associated thumps and thunderings approached.

Whatever was happening topside didn't sound fun. But

eventually the din fell behind them, and Chicken's emergency lighting turned from red to pinkish, brightening a few increments as the DONQ's sensors registered the change. Once Marge said—and Coyote's sense of direction concurred—they were wending eastward on the final half-klick, the runner called a halt, opened up Chicken's side panel and tapped in a few commands.

"That model ain't standard." Joe chewed on half a Jvstin bar—the last ration Coyote would give her cargo.

"One of a kind," Coyote allowed, and closed up, giving the double tap to lock everything. A few bugs in the DONQ-E's code were allowed to stay for a variety of reasons, not least as insurance against theft. "And doesn't ask to split the take."

"What you get paid for this, huh?"

None of your fucking business. "Askin a runner that's a good way to get left in the desert."

"We're close, though? He pointed upward, two swift jabs, his eyebrows raising. "That means we're close."

"Job's not done until we're over the border." Coyote showed her teeth. "Stow your trash and get your girlfriend on her feet."

A swift snarl passing over his face, stormveil masking distant mountains. "Korinna kept us together. In Distarritz."

And I fuckin got you out. "Then go return the favor and keep her moving, woof-woof."

Marge had also drifted close. "Fresh air coming in," she said in an undertone, as soon as Joe stamped away to minister to the drooping feline. "But…"

I knew it. There was always, *always* something at the end of a run. Coyote tore open her own ration—a full bar, she was gonna need it—and waited.

Finally, Margie shrugged. "I don't like how it smells."

"You smellin smoke? Lotta boom up there."

"Just that, I wouldn't say anything. But the rock says there's people out there–not like us, though. Armed and stupid."

"Rock called 'em stupid?" Coyote was going to have to revise her own personal estimation of geologic intelligence.

"My *nose* said they're armed." Margie was pale, her round pretty cheeks lightly floured with dust. "Rock says they're not shifters. Which means stupid."

Well, Coyote couldn't really argue with that. "Stupid still kills," she muttered. "'Course they're runnin patrols near the entrances. Rock say how many?"

"Nose says it's a few. And full daylight."

Coyote rocked back on her heels slightly, took her time chewing a huge mouthful of protein bar. Her teeth were finally near full remineralization, and she couldn't wait for a beer. Which was dangerous; some runners relaxed in sight of the goal.

A good way to get killed. She ran her tongue between top lip and incisors, getting everything nice and clean.

When she spoke, it was below mic threshold, not loud enough to reach the others. "You're smarter than you want anyone to know, *Margie*." Deliberate emphasis on the name.

"So're you, *Ky*." Marge returned the favor. "Don't think you're planning to sit in here and wait for the crowd to clear."

The corners of Coyote's lips wanted to twitch upward; she denied the motion, so far as she was able. "Where's the fun in that?" She popped the rest of the bar in, gave it two chews, and sent it down nearly whole.

Time to finish the run.

Chicken's lights dialed down to nothing as a faint glowing edge lit in the distance. Slowly, the rock walls slunk back into visibility, shadows lying differently since the light was natural and coming from the opposite direction. The front line was a growl to their backs, a giant creature torment-thrashing. Crackles and whistles preceded the deeper thumpcrumps of impact, but the sounds didn't hit in the gut anymore or shake thin strands of sand from the ceiling.

The border–or what had been the border before this offensive opened up–was still ahead. Right before the last bend–a ninety-degree angle, good for breaking the escape of working lights from within the honeycomb of tunnels– Coyote called another halt and gestured her cargo close.

"I go out first," she said, low but clear and distinct. "You keep your asses with Chicken until he starts to move. When he does you stay in his blur and hope to shit there's no Lindy drones looking to kamikaze the front line from this angle." That was a real wildcard; both runner and her cargo were entirely in the hands of luck and whatever shit-for-brains power looked out for shifters now. "You hunch, stay low, you run like hell. There's some gullies about three-quarters of a klick away, that's cover. Chicken will stop where he's supposed to and that'll mean you're out of small-arms range, but you keep going southwest until you hit the road. Stay in the ditch to the far left and if you hear fire, hide in the scrub. Road'll take you into town eventually, and Marge-in-charge'll get you to Fassby. You got it?"

A short, tense quiet. Sazi flinched as a set of shrieks in the middle distance announced a ressil-rocket strike; they were mopping up behind the leading edge. Looked like the front was no-shit moving, at long, long last.

Korinna took a gulp of the less-rancid air flooding around the corner. "What about you?"

"Patrols out there ain't gonna slow down to identify. It's shoot first don't ask–anything without Federal ping or flash gets vented. None of you fuckin fast or smart enough to play tag. So, you wait with Chicken until he starts to move. I ain't sayin it again."

Marge had gone pale. "You sure Fassby will..."

Coyote almost regretted the fact that she wasn't gonna see this shifter again. It was a goddamn delight to have cargo that could think a half-step ahead. "He knows I'll be along to check, Margie. Besides, he gets a kickback for every intel boost he passes along, and these shifters know about a Lindy high-up they've been tracking for a while."

News that Deranian had been in charge of Distarritz was high-value even after Federal intelligence found out the fucker was dead, and Coyote was betting that latter piece of gossip hadn't made it through the intel pipeline yet. It was also possible the camp was finally being emptied, shifters hooded and packed into whatever transport could be scrounged, the ungifted undesirables forced to march deeper into Lindyland as the front looked ready to crack.

Or maybe not, who could tell? Either way, these haggard survivors were worth a good bounty to Fassby. It was the last bit of help anyone would ever give them, above the border or below. But if they'd survived the cages, they had a chance.

A tingle spilled down Coyote's back, the instinct of a hunted creature about to draw pursuit away from den and pups.

She spun on a worn-down bootheel and darted around the corner, her eye squinting against the sudden assault of daylight.

Time to run.

PLAYTIME

She'd played grabass with Federal patrols plenty, especially on smuggling runs. Never this close to an active combat line, though, where they were singularly unwilling to be amused or lackadaisical–and where they could call in drone support.

Some scrub wranglers were just crazy enough to yell for heat despite the risk of catching a bombload themselves. There wasn't a lot of daylight between patrollers who hunted their opposing players in the wilderness and the runners slipping past or between both.

But every millimeter of that sunshine counted, at least to her.

Flat on her belly, peering through thorny scrub, her mouth gapped to take in low, slow breaths, Coyote tasted burning sage and creosote, dust and live fire, smoke and burning metal. Her ears rang, the higher registers of shifter hearing muffled until healing artillery-pierced drum membranes kicked in.

She'd attached all six soffa grenades wheeled out of Drood to her bandolier. Expensive as fuck, but nothing was quite so useful for distracting every patrol in the area. Loud and impressive, they fucked up even whisper-comms, and there were continual scares among the Fed high-ups that the Lindys had figured out that particular proprietary tech. Of course, if Coyote was caught with such rarefied items, it wasn't just jail but Federal brig before being "drafted" to a frontline battalion as shifter support.

The first pair of soffas was just for openers, getting the attention of nearby playmates. Coyote lobbed the second pair three seconds apart just in front of an approaching patrol before taking off, not bothering to duck so the dazed and ear-ringing half a dozen soldiers in real cowboy gear–patrollers weren't held to the same sartorial standard as spit-and-polish troops–could glimpse a shadow through the veils of flying sand and dust.

And *that* was why she wasn't so worried about her cargo being seen. Between the dust cloud of battle, Chicken's blur messing with any number of instrumental scans, and the soffas temporarily crack-womping every comm within five hundred meters, they were covered. Even senkas couldn't pierce this fog.

Of course, that meant Coyote had at least two staggering groups of Federals on her back, more on the way. It turned out there were multiple patrol units watching the various tunnel exits, and none of them were overjoyed by that kind of fire right on their patch. If they'd been a little farther apart they'd be chasing each other's tails for long enough to let the cargo slip by, but the groups had been too fucking close together and knowledge of Federal combat-sweep protocol, not to mention instinct, told her there *had* to be at least one more.

Chicken would have started moving at the first soffa blast. The cargo was exhausted and dazed, but if any situation would call out a final burst of speed and grace, this would be it.

Instinct spoke again and she was up and running before conscious thought arrived to tell her why. A change in air pressure, slight but definite, sent chills down arms and legs still striped with bruises and deep, angry-red furrows of shiny scar tissue. The bandage over her wounded eye slipped, the fringe on her jacket snapped like flags in high wind, and shadows loomed in the dust.

Move, bitch. Move fast, move now.

Eight-man squad, loaded with gear and moving with experienced calm. She emerged from the flying sand and her good hand flashed up, a heel-strike not to the center of the face—break nasal promontory and drive it into the brain—but under the chin, and she pulled the hit as well, not wanting to kill.

Just disable, hard.

They were Federals, after all. Not quite on her side—if she could be said to have one in all this madness—because even those who talked about "freedom" and "equality" could turn on shifters in a heartbeat and probably would once the war was over, the common enemy dealt with, and the fact that there were stronger, faster things superseding humanity on the evolutionary chain truly sank in. But for the moment, these soldiers might even believe what they said about fighting fash, about making the world safer for justice and equality.

Besides, there was no bounty on killing your own, from Drood or anyone else.

Second one got a kick right above the knee, between ceramo plates. A greenstick crack of breakage, a howl, a spatter of fire as someone on the flank figured out they were under attack but didn't realize it was an up-close threat instead of some dim shape in the smokeveil.

Dumbass. But they were, after all, ungifted. Too slow, even against a one-eyed, one-and-a-half-handed bitch reeling from Distarritz's loving embrace. She grabbed the third and shoved him into the fourth hard enough to knock both of their asses into semiconsciousness for the next ninety seconds at least, turned and leapt, her knee ramming into the chest of the fifth with a crunch different than artillery. Blood flew from the soldier's lip–he'd bitten it almost clean through, and ruby droplets hung on the air as he went down.

Coyote had to twist in midair to keep from landing on him, because a boot through his ribs would do more damage than she wanted. Hit the ground too hard, nearly fetching up against a looming boulder, rolling with a sideways twitch and freeing the fifth soffa from its strap-holder with a savage, perfectly calibrated yank. Popping the tab, tossing it over her shoulder, then she was low half-shift, weaving between thickening scrub and boulders, cutting across the hill before turning southward.

Others got turned around in soupcloud like this, but not her. Rock might talk to Margie, but Coyote had the wind. Air told her all she needed to know, even with her good eye nearly shut and her tongue lolling.

Crump. The soffa went off, and she hoped she'd flung it far enough to keep from taking out the patrollers left upright. With any luck they were down covering their wounded from a threat they had no idea was already hell and gone.

Just passin through, she might have murmured, but her half-shift snout wasn't built for the words and no howl or yip permitted to give away her location, or warn further prey lurking in the smoke.

Pressure changed again and Coyote responded instantly,

a burst of frantic speed. Gouts of sand were flung from her paws as she raced, and when the bolly landed–high explosive, lobbed from a massive crouching gun several kilometers away and falling short either because its charge was fuckered at the factory or some officer had shorted their calculation by a fraction of a digit–she was lifted and flung by a giant warm hand. Hit *hard*, bones snapping and the pain all through her like crimson wire.

Fucksake, survive Distarritz and get bombed by fucking Federals. It was funny, if you stopped to think about it.

Coyote didn't. The shift wracked her once more, running a single silver needle from crown to soles, every cell and hair brought into stinging focus. Cracked bone fused in a single messy seizure-burst, shredded muscles gripped, and a creature neither wholly human nor animal, intent only upon survival, staggered away from the shell crater which had swallowed the lives she had tried not to take.

The advance ground on.

SEE WHAT HAPPENS

Convoys moved through town in steady streams heading for the black northern horizon, distant thunder and flashes hammering at the fash. Breathless communiques hummed over the airwaves–there had been a breakthrough. Not here, of course.

Shit like that never happened here.

No, the real breaks were to east and west. They were rolling into Lindyland giant pincer-style, looking to grab the ideological heart of the Bloc. Lindbergh's grip on parts north, all the way to the prairie outposts guarding the front line of what was now southern Transcanada, was shaken for sure.

The bounty from Drood for the fash she could swear to killing didn't even cover three-quarters of the investment made in gear for the run, but she had the last soffa grenade and a few more bits of kit to keep, plus Chicken was in great shape even after weeks in the field. It was the closest thing to a pity fuck Coyote had ever granted, but that was all right. She'd taken the eyepatch off before she went into the silver loaf-shaped trailer, and showed the filthy-mouthed asshole her hand too.

Drood loved that shit. He listened to her highly edited account of springing a few shifters from a Lindy camp, and in return gave her all the current gossip and rumor for free over a pint of bathtub could-be-gin.

She was nearly caught by a draft detail getting back to the junkyard, and decided to stay low for a while.

It was good to eat when she felt like it. To wash the last of the sand from her hide and creases, to crack a sweating, ice-cold Hearne Lager from the fridge while she rested her battered boots on an ancient engine block, quite probably an ancestor of whatever mechanical bullshit propelled Deranian's car. The leftover twitches and flinching died down bit by bit, like they did after every bad run.

Best of all, the nightmares of the camp had stopped. Her dreams were still bloody, cruel, and full of horror... but she woke with relief, blinking in the dimness of her burrow, and when she emerged into the workshop, Chicken's oculars flashed briefly, verifying her biometrics. He sometimes champed his strong metal teeth thoughtfully before settling back into charging mode.

Maybe DONQ units dreamed. There was no way to ask.

She had a few credits saved even after the loss, and didn't have to take another run until the front calmed down. There would be a lot of anxious families wanting to find missing soldiers; one or two might be desperate enough to come looking for her. If all else failed there was materiel to lift from convoys, cargo needing transport in one direction or another, a wide and variable banquet in the cracks of what they called civilization.

A scavenger can always find a meal.

Or maybe Coyote was waiting, because after several days

of rest, she heard the footsteps outside while a glaring dusk was finishing its daily sun-strangling, as the artillery thunder grew intermittent. The noise of the slowly grinding offensive had become normal and thus ignored. Her ears were back in tiptop shape, and whoever was approaching made no attempt to be silent.

Which was probably wise, considering.

Coyote did not reach for the Federal sidearm strapped to her belt or the rifle propped nearby for home defense. Instead, she settled on a stool near the fridge, watching the door she'd once brought a fellow shifter through.

Margie's hair was freshly combed, her coveralls clean and pressed. Her nose twitched a little and she blinked twice, hunching well-rounded, muscular shoulders. Her boots were a different pair now; she'd kept the satchel and the weapons rig from their trip up north—though not the rifle. Getting caught with that would put her in a brig at best.

The most surprising addition to her attire was a jacket like Coyote's, though of far more ample dimension, due to her greater solidity. The fringe was shorter, but would still blur her outline in the desert.

She also carried a heavy glass bottle, glowing amber under the lighting strips. She stopped just inside the doorway, glancing at the bay where Chicken hung.

The DONQ's oculars flickered again. Coyote tapped her fingers on the railing next to her seat, a particular sonic pattern, and Chicken subsided. She said nothing, just tilted the lager bottle, filled her mouth with beer. Held the cold foaming, before letting it slide down her throat.

Margie blinked twice again. "Sorry to visit unannounced." A little defensively. "But you weren't at the Mudhole, Fassby doesn't know where you live, and the guy in the trailer–"

"Drood wouldn't say, even if he guessed." It wouldn't be smart, or conducive to business.

"So I thought, why not." Margie blinked again. "Kind of expected you to be gone."

"I like it here."

"It's nice." Margie cleared her throat. "The others are fine. You know they have therapy, for... for former camp..."

"Yeah." Coyote couldn't see the point, but then again, some people liked talking. The bottle's mouth was chill against her lower lip; she traced the curve slowly, thoughtfully. Waited.

"Whiskey." Margie lifted her own cargo. It was real old-style glass, heavy and blocky; the label was faded but looked legit. "Pre-war. The others kicked in some of the stipends they get–for reentry into society, the Feds say. They didn't believe you'd done it for only two hundred. How's Chicken?"

"Holding up," Coyote allowed. "You paid me, Margie. It's done."

"Well, about that." Margie took two steps farther into the garage, glanced around like she expected a tripwire mine to go off, took another. As if easing up on skittish prey. "We work well together. Right?"

Coyote lowered the beer bottle. "Not a lot of working on your part."

"I'm gonna overlook that remark." Margie straightened slightly, and glared at her. "So, what's the next job?"

Nothing yet, Coyote could have said, but that wasn't something you let a stranger know. "Oh, you want a cut?"

"Three reasons." The other shifter visibly made up her mind, set her chin, and set out across metal grate-flooring with a decided though quiet near-shuffle step, her fine round hips rolling gracefully. The fringe moved nice on her curves, really. "I hate the fash. I want to hurt 'em any way I can."

Oh, great. A crusader. "War's gonna end sometime." Maybe sooner rather than later, if the Fed propaganda was even a third true. Transcanada was supposedly squeezing from farther north, and word said even Cascadia was tired of the bullshit despite taking a cut of any blockade-running trickling Lindyward through their ports.

"And when it does I want to survive," Margie said. "So does Nat, but she's not cut out for this."

"No she is not," Coyote agreed. "What's reason three?"

"Reason three." Margie had reached the counter. She pulled out the other stool, the one Coyote never used because it was a little too low for comfort, and set the bottle on the varnished surface. "Yeah. Three. Well, you see, I think I like you."

What. The fuck. Coyote eyed the other woman. "You paid me," she said, as gently as possible. "Chicken's running fine. Sometimes cargo gets feelings, but–"

"I'm not *cargo.*" A dangerous glint in Margie's dark eyes. "My kind knows what we like, Ky."

Ky. It sounded nice. Coyote still shook her head. "I'm a real bitch, Margie."

"Oh, I know." And the other shifter laughed, giving her head a pert little toss. The stripe glowed, undyed and proud. "Spent enough time with you to prove it."

Coyote shrugged. She reached for the bottle, tipped it this way and that, admiring the sheen on the liquid inside. Prewar, expensive, antique. Either Margie had lifted it, or she'd done work for someone who had access.

"You're not gonna rip my spine out through my asshole if I say no, are you?"

"Go ahead. Say no." Margie's grin was nearly triangular, and very fetching. "See what happens."

"Fuck." Coyote lifted the bottle, cracked the lid with a

quick twist. It was good to have both hands functional again. "Guess we're drinkin. I don't have a job lined up yet."

"That's okay." The badger shifter's smile widened. "We've got some time."

THE END

(...UNTIL THE NEXT DAMN JOB.)

ACKNOWLEDGEMENTS

Thanks are first and foremost due to Kevin Hearne, who invited me to the dance and let me move as the music bid. Much gratitude is also due to Phineas X. Jones, who did the impossible to catch Coyote; and to the Marvelous Editrix for thoughtful, endlessly useful editing.

As always, I am grateful for my children, who patiently listen to me babble about imaginary worlds. Last but not least, dear Reader, I must thank *you*–and let me do so in the way we both like best, by telling you another story.

Soon.

ABOUT THE AUTHOR

Lilith Saintcrow resides in the rainy Pacific Northwest with her children, dogs, cat, and library for wayward texts.

www.lilithsaintcrow.com

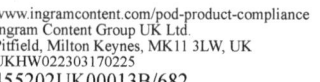